*if
you are afraid
of heights*

Also by Raj Kamal Jha

THE BLUE BEDSPREAD

RAJ KAMAL JHA

if you are afraid of heights

HARCOURT, INC.

Orlando   Austin   New York   San Diego   Toronto   London

Requests for permission to make copies of any part
of the work should be mailed to the following address:
Permissions Department, Harcourt, Inc.,
6277 Sea Harbor Drive, Orlando, Florida 32887-6777.

www.HarcourtBooks.com

First published in the United Kingdom by Picador

Library of Congress Cataloging-in-Publication Data
Jha, Raj Kamal, 1966–
If you are afraid of heights/Raj Kamal Jha.—1st U.S. ed.
p.   cm.
ISBN 0-15-101109-5
1. India—Social life and customs—Fiction.   I. Title.
PR9499.3.J49I35 2004
823'.914—dc22   2004007301

Printed in the United States of America

First U.S. edition
A C E G I K J H F D B

*To my father Munishwar Jha and
my mother Ranjana Jha*

Deep down, I don't believe it takes any special talent for a person to lift himself off the ground and hover in the air. We all have it in us – every man, woman, and child . . . You must learn to stop being yourself. That's where it begins, and everything else follows from that.

Paul Auster, *Mr Vertigo*

THE FIRST PROLOGUE

Look at the picture on the cover, there's a child, a girl in a red dress; there's a bird, a crow in a blue white sky. And then there are a few things you cannot see.

One: The child is between eleven and twelve years of age. She's standing on the balcony of a two-room flat in a building that, from the street outside, looks like a crying face. Its windows are the eyes, half-closed by curtains, smudged and wrinkled. Rain, wind and sun of countless years have marked the wall, streaking it in several lines, two of which look like lines of tears, one falling below each window. The mouth is the balcony, curved down under the weight of iron railings, rusted and misshapen. Like the stained teeth of someone very sad. And someone very old.

Two: The balcony, where the child stands, leads into a room behind her. This is where she sleeps on a single bed against the wall. This room – because there are only two rooms in the house – serves as a living room for most of the day. It has chairs, a potted plant, a second-hand table in the centre with a cracked glass top on which are kept some of the child's school books, one opened in the middle.

Three: The child is crying. Tears fill her eyes and

perhaps that's why she sees the crow as blurred, that's why she can't see me.

Four: I'm sitting on the crow's back, my legs pressed hard against its sides, my body raised so that the bird doesn't feel my weight.

Since morning, I have flown in circles across the sky and over the city, throughout the day, the afternoon and the evening, watching the child's father and mother. I have swooped down several times, in between the tram wires, over the tops of trees, the terraces of buildings, once even below an aircraft descending to land. For a few hours, when it poured this morning, I caught the rain in my eyes, high up, clear and cold, before it mixed with the dust blown up by the shuffle of feet from the streets below. Sometimes, I got off the bird's back to walk or stand still so that I could get a better look at her parents. And sometimes, just to give the poor little bird a break.

Now I'm flying down to meet the child because I have something to show her, I have something to tell: pictures I have taken, words I have scribbled.

What happens when I land, what do the child and I do, we shall come to all of that later – much later, in fact, right at the end when we shall let the child do the talking.

As of now, let's change the blue white morning of the sky to a deep purple evening. Because it's in the dying light of day that our story begins.

The curtains grow dark, the light from the street lamps outside dapples their fabric, making the yellow more yellow, the edges of the balcony sharper, much sharper than they appear on the cover. As if they were etched in cement with a thick, black pencil.

In the room behind the child, sits her father.

Father's of medium height, medium age, medium weight, medium nose, medium eyes, everything medium. Even in colour he's medium brown. Like wood left outside in the heat and the rain.

He's just back from work, from the City Building Clearance Office where his job is to sit at the front desk, receive construction plans from those who want to build new houses in this crumbling city.

He files their papers, makes a note in the register every time he gets a plan and then he passes it on to those who have to decide whether any rules have been broken. And, if yes, what the fine should be.

Father is taking his shoes off.

In the next room, Mother is setting up dinner. She has hair like her daughter, dark and straight.

As Father rolls his socks, puts them into his shoes, one by one, he can smell the city on his feet. He bends down to pick the shoes up, to take them to the corner of the room where all the shoes and the slippers lie, in one neat row.

From the next room, he can hear dishes being put on the table, water being poured into glasses, the sound of dinner being served. He walks out of the room to wash up – he can smell the city on his hands as well.

In the bathroom, there's no water in the tap so he scoops a mug from the bucket and rinses his hands, his feet and his mouth making a noise that echoes off the red cement wall and the white toilet bowl, both stained, cracked in several places.

He looks into the mirror at his face, wet, turns back, switches off the lights and walks towards the dining table. And in that ten-, eleven-step walk, which is the journey from the bathroom to the dining table, Father thinks he hears the sound of a child crying and he closes his eyes once – for slightly longer than a blink.

At least, that's what it looks like, from the heights where I am.

PART ONE

of heights

Once upon a time in the city

ONCE UPON A TIME in the city, there lived a woman called Rima and a man named Amir and late one night, they met in an accident, face to face, she picked out the shards of broken glass from his face, they fell in love and just when it seemed they were settling down to live happily ever after, a strange little thing happened one night: Rima woke up hearing a child cry.

She couldn't make out if it was a boy or a girl because it was a wail, rising and falling, loud and soft, sometimes high-pitched, sometimes low, broken here and there by small hiccups from what could only have been a small chest. She got up from the bed, her pillow slipped to the floor, its thud too soft to wake Amir; she drew the drapes aside and looked this way and that, right and left, but saw nothing. Except, of course, the black night, the black street. And a dog.

Brown. She could make out two white patches on its neck where something had chewed at its fur. Its tail was little more than a stump. It must have fallen asleep under a parked taxi right in front of its rear wheels and the driver must have reversed without looking, shearing a bit off the tail.

Such accidents happen every day in this city.

Rima watched the dog lap at the black water in the drain, sniff and sift whatever floated by, sit down, scratch an itch. There was no traffic at that hour so the dog curled up in the middle of the road itself and lowered its head between its paws. By the time it closed its eyes, the child's crying had stopped.

Rima went back to bed, Amir still fast asleep.

When she woke up the next morning, she had forgotten the crying. Only once or twice during the afternoon, when she dropped something small, insignificant, maybe a hairpin, perhaps a rubber band, and then bent down to pick it up, did the crying return. Then she noticed it: the crying returned when Amir was in the room; when he walked away from her, it was as if the crying would fade, get softer and softer with each step he took. So that when he left the room, the crying became a strain of sound from some place far, far away, carried by a wind so light she could hardly feel it. It stayed in her ears for such a fleeting moment that it scarcely registered, neither in thought nor in feeling.

But that night, with Amir next to her in bed, the whole sequence of the previous day repeated itself. The crying began, she found herself walking to the window and looking out. Once again, there was nothing except the wail and the dog, the same dog, but this time running after something imaginary, stopping, turning back, running again before it sat down and went to sleep.

Again the crying stopped, again she returned to bed.

From the second morning, however, Amir stayed at home right through and there was no escaping the crying. She woke up with the sound as if sometime during the night, after she had gone back to sleep, the child had crawled into her ear to sit deep inside, curled up, like some stubborn foetus, fully formed but refusing to leave, clutching tight her nerves and her bones, clawing, scraping her eardrum with its fingers, muffling all other sounds in the house.

It's my fault, Rima told herself, it's got nothing to do with Amir being here. This is just like when water enters the ear, when I am in the shower or in the rain, no more, no less. So what do I need to do? I need to give my head a good, hard jerk, maybe hop on one leg, tilt my head, yes I'll look funny, who cares?

But that didn't help.

Forget it, she said. I'll get used to it, sooner rather than later the crying will dribble out into other sounds: Amir pouring water into a glass, the TV from the house upstairs, the boy playing cricket with his maid in the yard below.

That didn't help either.

For six full days, she heard it in her head. And for the next six nights, she woke up to hear the crying from the street outside. On the seventh morning, she thought: let me tell Amir, see what he says.

He didn't say much. Tell me when you hear it, he said. Wake me up, I'll listen too.

So that night, she woke him up even before the crying had begun and they both stood by the window, Amir and Rima, his hand on her right shoulder. He could see and feel the goosebumps on her neck, smell the shampoo in her hair against his chin. Her hair fell to her shoulders in one smooth wave, but one strand, or two, had broken free in her sleep. This was distracting since it tickled his chin, making him move back a bit, a fraction of an inch, and gently blow at the hair.

She didn't feel a thing and, thus settled, they watched and waited.

A City Transport Corporation bus passed, red, its colour running, the No Standing sign glowing on its sides. A truck trundled by, a foreign-made truck, as long as a block of houses, with brand new Korean cars in wooden crates stacked in two rows of almost a dozen each. A giant made of metal lying on his side, smiling in the night, the cars his teeth, the crates his braces. Two men walked by, talking, one coughed, the other laughed, the one who coughed was drunk since his feet walked in a direction he didn't want to go, the laughing man kept nudging him back, they both turned round the corner. And then the crying began.

Listen, Rima whispered with a shiver. It's the same sound, the same rise and fall, the same breaths. Like someone's recorded it on a sophisticated tape, the kind they use in radio stations, and is now hiding in the shadows, playing the cassette. Trying to scare me.

Don't worry, said Amir. There are a thousand and one reasons in this city for children to cry. Why don't we talk about this in the morning, why don't we go back to sleep?

Rima said no, I need to find out who this child is, why does it cry, I don't want to wake up every night like this and I don't want this sound in my ear during the day.

What she didn't tell him, because she didn't wish to,

was that she wanted to find out if the crying stopped when she left Amir.

So what do you want to do? he asked.

I'll go check the street below, walk a few steps up and down and then come back. The child can't be far away.

You want me to come with you? Amir said.

No, don't worry, she said, I'll be back in a few minutes.

OK, take an umbrella, it was raining the whole day today. Be careful, he said.

I will, she said.

He heard her walk to the other room, open the steel cupboard, he heard the noise of the aluminium hangers bumping into each other, the rustle of her dresses as she searched for something to wear.

He heard the cupboard door close, the click, the latch fall into place; the sound of her fingers against her face as she applied some cream; he heard the plastic bottle being put down on the dressing table; the main door open and close; the sound of her footsteps as she walked down the two flights of dark stairs to the street below. And all this while, Amir waited in bed, the window still open, thinking things entirely unconnected to what was happening around him.

Like how Rima looked when she bent down to open the fridge and take out a bottle of water, how its green light lit her face and her neck.

Or, how every once in a while, her hands strayed, on their own, towards her face, to tuck the hair behind her right ear. And the waffle pattern on her cheeks when she fell asleep on the chair, her face pressed against the cane lattice of its backrest.

Thinking such things, Amir began to slide back into sleep unaware that, in the blink of an eye, it would all be over. The city, this part of the earth, would turn, would begin to leave the moon and meet the sun. Unaware that Rima had left, never to return.

Leaving him behind, alone, and for company, the sound of a child crying.

This is the story, in brief.

But it needs to be told in full, if only to understand how, out of all the men, women and children in this city, sixteen million at last count, it had to be Amir and Rima, two people whose names are mirror reflections of each other, who met in the accident, face to face, amid shards of broken glass.

So we need to, as the story takes its course, pick up details strewn along the way. Often the obvious, sometimes the obscure. Like a power cut in the neighbourhood and Amir's kerosene lamp. Or his job at the post office, the stains in his cracked toilet. Or how, trying to remove them with acid one day, he splashed some on his hand, peeling off a thin layer of skin that left permanent white blotches on two of his fingers.

What does all this have to do with Rima? Or with the morning, afternoon, evening and, finally, the night of that fateful accident? For an answer, we should begin before Rima and Amir ever met.

Long before they ever met

LONG BEFORE Rima and Amir ever met, there came up in this city a building called Paradise Park. It was a special building, a building so special that if you stopped anyone on the street, man, woman or child, hungry or well fed, half-naked or well dressed, asked them, *Excuse me, which way is Paradise Park?* right there, in front of your eyes, you would see them change. You would see them lower their heads in respect, their eyes in fear, look you over from head to toe. Do little things that would make you feel special, sometimes even make you squirm.

For example, if it were day and the sun was high and hot, like in May or June, they would take a few steps front or back to give you a bit of their shadow. So that you were sheltered from the heat.

If it were raining, July, August, and if they had an umbrella, big and black, and you didn't, they would tip it so that you didn't get wet.

And if it were a winter evening, long and cold, when V-neck sweaters served little purpose, when woollen mufflers did nothing except make your ears itch, they would shuffle, adjust themselves, so that they didn't block the light from the street lamp above, instead let it fall directly on you, give you some extra warmth.

And then, when you were comfortable, they would answer your question without speaking much. They would only raise their hands, you could see the dirt in their nails, the wrinkles on their fingers, and by the time you were ready to thank them, they would have left for home.

Perhaps to tell their loved ones: Today I met someone who stopped me to ask *Excuse me, which way is Paradise Park?*

That's how special Paradise Park was.

It was the tallest building in the city. There were other tall buildings: Skyview Heights, the office complex with a revolving restaurant at the top but that wasn't high enough. For if you looked down, you could easily see the bald patch on a man's head below. A brown speck in a tiny black circle.

There was Himalaya Palace, a hotel so tall people stood on the street to look up whenever they wanted to cure the stiffness in their necks.

But Paradise Park was Paradise Park.

This was almost the real thing, like the ones they have in pictures, buildings that reach so high you don't know where their shadows end or begin. Skyscrapers, whose roofs scrape chips of cloud off the sky which then float down, cushioned by the wind, and come to rest hanging in mid-air. Hugging the windows day and night, like fog does on some winter mornings.

So unique was its construction that no one knew how many floors it had. Or for that matter, how many people lived there. Even if you tried, you couldn't count since the building rose like a giant cylinder, smooth on its outside surface, no lines marking the floors or the windows. Some said if you lived on each floor for a week, starting from the ground, it would take you two full years to reach the roof. That makes it fifty-two times two, one hundred and four floors but this sounds too pat. After all, this was just one of the stories about the building that went around the city. From one ear to the other in a game of Chinese whispers played, unwittingly, by sixteen million people.

The favourite one, though, was the story of the sea and the gulls. And it went like this:

Each floor on Paradise Park had only one apartment, and one side of its living room was a wall made entirely of glass, the kind of glass they use in telescopes. So that on nights when the sky was clear, when the wind had blown away the dust and the smoke, when the moon and the stars were in their right places, exerting just that precise gravitational pull, you could see the Bay of Bengal, which is at least five hundred miles away, right outside the living room. So sharp was this lens-window that you could see the waves, the green foam, the white spray breaking across the shore, crashing against the wall.

You could even see, if you were lucky, little crabs left behind by the water flailing their legs, trying to hold on to the shifting sand. Or a fisherman and his family dragging their net across the sand, the children picking up the fish that fell through the sieves, a motor boat gliding in the distance.

And because sound cannot be telescoped, the whole thing was silent. When the gulls flew, you could see them through the glass, their yellow beaks parting, their white wings flapping, but you heard nothing. Only gentle, silent noises: your fingers against the glass, the edge of a curtain catching the draft from the air conditioner, sometimes a child crying outside.

A third story was about how the driveway in Paradise Park was so clean you could eat off it. You only had to mark out your plate with chalk, pile up the rice, lay out the vegetables, even the chicken or the fish, take a spoon, tap some mango pickle in the top left-hand corner, let the curry run on the concrete – it didn't matter. You felt not a single speck of grit between your teeth.

Well, it's here that our story takes place because this is where Rima lived and where she brought Amir on the night of the accident.

He lay, hurt and half-conscious, on the driveway, and it was from there that he got his first view of Paradise Park. With pain's rough tongue licking the deep cuts on his face, he saw a spotless strip of black concrete, Rima's feet, her shoes, black with buckles, as she walked up and down, waiting for the guard to give her the keys so that she could help him get up, get into the lift, bring him into her house.

He saw her ankles, her crumpled blue sari, a loose thread from its hem, the fabric highlighting the shape of her shin. He smelled her wrists as she bent down to adjust his shirt, brush a blade of grass caught in his hair. And then, crouching, she put her arm under his and said, get up, let me know if it hurts. He got up, leaning on her, her hair against his chin, and they both walked into her home in Paradise Park.

Over the next few weeks she nursed him with care, and later with what seemed like some kind of love. She got doctors who treated the discoloured surfaces of his wounds while she looked deeper to find and cure ailments he never knew existed. She asked him questions and he gave her answers, first in half-sentences, broken words, then with more confidence, wrapping them with ribbons of politeness and gratitude.

And thus, day by bright day, night by shimmering night, Amir began to settle into his new life, high above the city where he once lived but now could see only through the glass of the window and the dreams of his sleep.

Paradise Park: a brief history

PARADISE PARK went up right in the centre of the Maidan, which, in the language of this city, means a sprawl of empty land. The Maidan is an almost perfect circle, slightly over three miles in diameter, covered with grass, more brown than green, except in a few patches where, for some reason, nothing grows except dust and mud, where water collects in tiny ponds, still and dark, not even ankle deep. There are trees, not many, mainly banyan, whose branches grow down to become trunks of new trees, some eucalyptus, a flame of the forest here and there, a few palm trees that stand out. Just like that.

In one corner of the Maidan is an old Russian tank the army abandoned after they won the Bangladesh war more than thirty years ago, and left there as some sort of a memento. Once upon a time there must have been a ceremony here to which a VIP would have been invited, since there's a small board right next to the tank and a barbed wire fence that runs all around. But the letters on the board are illegible, washed away, smudged. The fence is cut in several places and these cuts aren't fresh, their edges have rusted a deep red, long tinged with black.

A dog lives in the tank's turret, its tail little more than a stump, birds rest here on their way home, their droppings crusted on the iron. In the evening, children come here to play from slums across the road where the river runs shallow, brown and heavy, weighed down by the pus of sick factories, dying one by one. While the children hide and seek in and around the tank, their mothers wipe the dust off and drape their clothes, wet and dripping, over the gun to dry.

In short, this is no park carefully maintained, well laid out. No benches and pathways, no trees arranged in precise rows or pretty flowers in neat hedges, pruned and trimmed every other day. In fact, if you are new to the city, one look at the Maidan and you know that this is an accident, as if centuries ago the city's builders and planners forgot about this sprawl, and by the time they realized that a little bit of space was left vacant, they were too tired to do anything. So they said let it lie, it won't do anybody any harm.

Now this is the only open space there is in a city where people live, five or six to one room, fifty or sixty to a bus stop, more than a thousand to a neighbourhood, these numbers increasing every day and every night.

That's why people come here, slipping out of their homes, whenever they get the chance, out of their bedroom, which is also the living room, which is also the dining room, away from the sound of a child crying, get into buses, and with their clothes wrinkled, wet with the sweat of strangers, they walk across the Maidan to watch the sky above, feel the grass below. Knowing that there's no one to either their left or right. They sit down without even looking, not bothered at all as to what happens to their trousers, their saris – will the mud stick or will it stain? – as they look into the distance, at nothing in particular, their tired eyes running over the city's skyline unchanged ever since they were born. The Grand Hotel, its glass windows yellow from the light of the lamps inside. The blinking neons of movie posters. Giant ads of filter-tipped cigarettes balanced between a woman's lips, each as long as a man sleeping. Baby food for a baby as big as a bus.

Newspapers called the Maidan the dying city's last lung, until one day, which is around the time our story begins, real-estate agents pulled up in small, white Korean cars, got out with a cellphone in one hand, a cigarette in the other, wearing white trousers and white T-shirts stretched tight over their gym-cured chests, their hair oiled but not greasy, their dark glasses hiding from the world all their eyes could see or show. And these men in white began to buy.

Whom they bought the land from, whom they paid, how much in cheque how much in cash, nobody knows because most of the transactions were, to use a common phrase, under the table.

The Maidan was what's called a protected area under the City Preservation Act of 1972. But like all laws across the world, it had loopholes so tiny you didn't even know they were there until you met lawyers with trained eyes and nimble fingers who could squeeze an entire herd of elephants through if only you gave them enough money.

These men had enough money, the officers at the City Building Clearance Office had pockets, deep and wide open. And so in less than a month, patches of the Maidan began to disappear. Into what, at first, seemed fairly innocuous.

'Dragon Chilli', a Chinese restaurant which gave fortune cookies with numbers written instead of your future. A woman's hairdresser called 'Madonna Clips' where they had magazines from London to choose your hairstyle from, their covers and pages creased so hard that all the models' faces and their hair were streaked with lines of white. A greetings-card store called 'Maidan Wishes', the *a* written as @ because it had a computer, Pentium inside, where, for ten rupees extra, you could get a four-line Happy Birthday poem, its last line rhyming with the name of your choice.

For example, if you typed in *Rima,* it would print out:

> *Happy Birthday to you,*
> *Happy Birthday to you,*
> *Happy Birthday dear Rima,*
> *Who's my best friend near and far*

Or something like that.

Then came Paradise Park.

It was like nothing the city had seen before.

Angry adjectives vanished from protesting newspapers as if they were printed in disappearing ink. Reporters broke into poetry, sought similes, mixed metaphors. Magazines ran photo-features on the construction machinery that worked through the night: hydraulic excavators and bulldozers, loaders and lifts, trucks and cranes, crushers and heavy earth-movers. All painted a bright yellow and a brighter red, sparkling under the glare of high-wattage lamps, lighting up the hills of sand and cement that made the site look like a desert, a mountain, a movie set, all of the above.

Cranes hummed the whole day, lifting all kinds of rods and buckets. Excavators kept chomping at the ground, gulping the grass and the earth, gargling slurry and stone, spitting tons of mud and concrete and then washing everything down with tar and cement.

Most of the work went on at night, and to ensure that the city got a surprise, like they do in foreign countries, they draped a huge sheet of thick plastic over the scaffolding so that in the morning you couldn't make out anything. Sometimes, when the wind blew hard, you could bend down, take a peek, see a bit of what was being built. A rectangle of a gleaming floor, one or two sunken lights, a lift shaft that rose endlessly into the sky.

Once in a while, a crow flew in, got lost in the maze of the steel girders, and from outside, if you looked carefully, you could see the thick plastic cover quiver, tremble as the bird hit against its surface, trying to get out.

Paradise Park is like a beautiful flower, said one writer, *dropped in a sewer, the sludge flowing past, its petals untainted. So strong is this flower's fragrance,* he went on, *that it overwhelms the stink, the rats and the waste, the rotting garbage that our callous authorities so loftily turn their noses up at.*

Another newspaper tried to be more lyrical: *Imagine a morgue, the room in the hospital that's full of corpses. Now think of a little child learning to walk. Place the child on the cold floor of this morgue, stand at the door and watch. Paradise Park is like this baby, taking its first steps in a room full of corpses. Let's celebrate new life in this dying city.*

In one corner of this dying city

AND IN ONE CORNER of this dying city, a forty-minute bus-ride away from the Maidan, lives Amir, in a two-room flat in a building that, from the street outside, looks like a crying face: its windows are the eyes, half-closed by curtains, smudged and wrinkled; the rain, wind and sun of countless years have marked the wall, streaked several lines, two of which look like tears, one below each window. The mouth is the balcony, curved down under the weight of iron railings, rusted and misshapen. Like the stained teeth of someone old, and someone very sad.

There's some irony here since the word 'Amir' means a rich man. Not to say that Amir is poor. In fact, compared to many in the city, even in his neighbourhood, he gets along pretty well: he works at the post office which pays him a little over five thousand rupees per month, consolidated. With an annual increment of about two hundred rupees, dearness allowance extra.

He is an EDA, an Extra Departmental Agent. This is a government job but it isn't a permanent one. In other words, of the dozen staff in his office, three women and nine men, his is the first one that will go if the government decides to cut costs, lay off. The flip side, however, is that Amir can, legally, work at a second job. Which he does.

So in the post office, he puts in eight hours a day, nine to five, Monday to Friday, second Saturdays off plus all national holidays. And five evenings a week, for another thousand a month, he teaches the daughter of Mr A. Sarkar, the Assistant Postmaster, his Boss at the office. The child is between eleven and twelve years old.

Six thousand rupees isn't a lot of money but Amir is, as the cliché goes, a man of modest means.

His wardrobe, if one may use so fancy a word, has two pairs of trousers, both black; two white shirts; a third blue with red checks; and a pair of shoes, black with steel buckles.

It helps that the trousers are black, especially in winter, since the colour hides the dirt and the grime for several days. In summer as well, when the water and the wind boil together in the sun, leaving behind sweat rings on clothes, around the knees and over the thighs. Because his trousers are black, he can see them just when they begin to form. This early warning helps, he wipes them away with water so that there's no need to wash the trousers, at least for a week.

His toilet bowl is white, cracked in several places where his shit gets stuck so that even though he pours in half a bottle of acid every other morning, the stains don't go away. When he first moved in, this made him angry, so angry that one day he poured in an entire bottle, splashing some acid on his hand. A thin layer of skin peeled off leaving permanent white blotches on two of his fingers. He soon realized, however, that his anger was not only misplaced, it was futile. For, he hardly had any visitors – there was no one to see the stains.

And even if anyone dropped by, it was only for a couple of minutes or so, a postman with a letter, the landlord's son with the rent bill – visitors who waited outside, never entered his house, far less use his toilet.

Amir pays two hundred and forty rupees as rent every month thanks to the City Tenancy Act of 1912 due to which rates haven't changed in the last twenty years, forcing the house owners to strike back in their own petty little ways.

Perhaps, that's why the pump that supplies water to his flat is switched off for most of the day and the light bulb in the staircase is rarely replaced. During the rain, water leaks through the broken panes in the windows, his cement floor is cracked like skin in winter, there is sparking in his switchboard since the fuse wire is too thin, it blows at least twice every week.

At night, there are other little problems. Cockroaches crawl out of the drain on his balcony which Amir has covered with a bucket full of water. He uses a heavy bucket but that hardly helps, for the insects squeeze themselves out, through the narrow gap between the bulge of the bucket's plastic and the floor.

Before turning in for the night, Amir pours water down the drain, a lot of water from a reasonable height, hoping that the force of the fall will make the insects lose their footing, push them down into the darkness. But in less than fifteen minutes, by the time he has returned to his room, the cockroaches have climbed back up to just below the drain, their antennae wet and glistening.

The first thing Amir does in the morning is to pick up two plastic buckets and go stand in line at the Municipal

Corporation hydrant, right below his house. His buckets full, he carries them back up two flights of stairs, splashing and spilling until he reaches his door, the stairs wet, his breath short, his calves hurting.

Every day, he has to make at least two trips, he needs that much water since he's never sure when the pump will be switched off, when the tap will run dry, whether he will have enough until the next morning. So he stores the water in containers of all kinds: teacups, the kettle, glasses, sometimes even the empty jars in which once he kept spices, salt and pepper.

The water arranged for, he cleans the lantern.

It's a glass belljar that fits into a metallic base into which he pours kerosene before wetting the adjustable wick. Usually, the soot on the glass can be wiped away with a dry piece of cloth but at least once a week, normally on Sundays, he uses soap, water and cloth and then just to make sure, he lets it dry in the sun. He likes to keep the lamp gleaming, ready for the power cut.

Long ago, the City Electric Supply Corporation used to publish a load-shedding schedule, one full page in the newspaper, in which they mentioned which units of which power-stations would be switched off and for how long. Based on this, they prepared a chart, perforated along the edges. They even printed pictures of tiny black scissors so that people would know where to tear, how to fold and then paste the chart on their walls. It gave the weekly timetable of power cuts in the city with a one-line intro-duction: *We are pleased to do this so that our valuable consumers can adjust their daily lives.* For some reason, now they have stopped doing this.

Instead, they disconnect the power supply as and when they wish so Amir has to be prepared. He has trained himself to detect when the supply will be back. When it will take minutes, when it will stretch into hours.

If everything is off, even the street lights, there's hope because they can't have so much blackness all around for so long a time. But the ones he's really wary of are what he calls the unfair power cuts: when one side of the street has all the lights on, only the other is dark. Or worse, when his is one of the few houses without power. This usually means that there's something wrong with the transformer at the substation, a 'local fault' which never gets fixed quickly unless you are lucky.

To prepare himself better for such nights, Amir has devised a little game, based on a principle of his own making: if you expect the worst, you are never disappointed.

So whenever there's a power cut in the evening, he goes around the house, turning all the switches off – those for the lights and the fans – convincing himself that he doesn't expect the supply to be restored anytime soon. Then he goes and sits on the balcony.

If it's early in the evening, he watches the trams and the buses go by, the trucks with the foreign cars stacked in rows. Begins counting. Or if it's late in the night, when there isn't anything to watch, he lies in bed and sometimes uses his fingers to shadow-draw on the wall: a dog barking, a duck, a fish, two rabbits fighting.

Or watches the shapes the plant makes, a tiny palm

tree which he keeps in an earthen pot in the living room. Somewhere a child cries, perhaps irritated by the heat and the darkness. He stares at the white streaks the acid has left behind on his fingers, and wonders how long will it be before the white skin turns brown again.

And it's while sitting still, allowing time to flow over him like water, that he suddenly notices – from the white haze outside his window, from the lights of the flat above him, the yellow strip on his bed – that the power supply is back.

It's only then that he gets up to switch the fan on, and listening to its loose wire make a noise against the motor, he falls asleep, the breeze drying the sweat that has collected during the darkness, behind his shoulders, on his neck, the crook of his arm, beneath his knee.

He is happy, his belief vindicated, convinced that the power is back only because he never expected it to be, because he turned all the switches off.

That's how Amir thinks.

As for what he looks like, where he's come from and what he does, we can wrap that up in a couple of short questions and answers:

What does Amir look like?

There's not much to say, let's put it this way: if you live in this city and you cross Amir in the street or you turn sideways to let him pass in some narrow lane, you won't look at him a second time. He's medium height, medium age, medium weight, medium nose, medium eyes, everything medium. Even in colour, he's medium brown, like wood left outside, for a couple of days, in the sun and the rain.

Where has he come from?

No one in the neighbourhood is sure; they know only that he suddenly showed up one morning, with one suitcase, walking confidently, as if he'd been living here for ever and had returned home after a break. Sometimes people see him walking with a bag, once in a while they can make out that he is carrying something that looks as if it's for a child: a chocolate bar, a tube of toothpaste which comes with a free rubber toy.

Is he married? Does he have a wife, a child?

No one knows.

In a city where, even if you shut them away, families squeeze themselves into any chink they can find, where children cry to be heard above the noise, where people, even those dead and long gone, sit on walls, curling the edges of their photographs with their hot, invisible breaths, steaming the glass frame, Amir is pretty much able to keep to himself. Silently, he prides himself on this achievement.

Who are his neighbours?

Quite a few but we can whittle the list down. There's the cobbler who sits on the pavement, just in front of the hydrant, with his shoeshine box, whom Amir likes to watch on some evenings, the way he daubs the white cream on the black shoe to make it shine. Or the way he runs his wrinkled fingers over the leather to check if he has hammered the nail to the right depth.

There are the two Shah brothers who run a snack shop and a telephone kiosk. They have a small TV set which they switch on whenever there is a cricket match so that people waiting in line to use the phone have something to watch while they wait.

'Das and Sons' is the sweet shop run by Mr Das himself who is always bare to the waist except from late November to February. He gets his children to work at the shop after school, the daughter folds the cardboard to make boxes, the son washes the earthen cups in which he sells curd. Amir sees both children in the morning, standing in line, usually behind him, at the Corporation tap.

Then there is Bomba. A ten-year-old boy, almost half Amir's height but double his weight, Bomba lives with his parents in the house upstairs. Every evening, Amir sees him drag his maid, a short, thin wisp of a girl, out to play cricket. He asks her to bowl to him and he keeps on batting, even when she bowls him out a dozen times or more.

What does Amir do in his spare time?

Most evenings, he takes the bus to Park Street, walks down right up to where it turns into Free School Street where once a week he visits a prostitute. Then he boards the late-night tram that trundles in a sweeping arc around the Maidan so that resting his face against one side of the wooden window, the frame cold to his forehead, he can see, across the blackness of the empty expanse and over the tops of the trees, scattered and still, the shimmering skyline of the city.

And set against it, the hulking shadows of machines crawling between the hills of sand and cement, rapidly putting together the rectangles, the squares and the circles of Paradise Park, the tallest building in the city.

What does he do at the post office?

Let's enter the post office and look at him as he sits in one corner, in his chair, at a desk to the left of the entrance, near the iron door.

The chair is brown, moulded plastic, with iron legs, the desk is made of plywood. It's here that he writes letters for those who can neither read nor write. Every day. As on the morning of the accident when he will meet Rima and everything will change for ever.

The post office

OR

The morning of the accident

SHIMLA POST OFFICE, zip code seven zero zero zero zero six, is where Amir arrives, exactly two minutes before opening time, this morning. The entrance to the post office has no awning, no shade, it's flush with the pavement, there's not even a single step above or below which means that if it's raining hard and you happen to pass by, need to stop for shelter, you take one step inside and you are right in the small waiting area, at the end of which are the counters, their glass panels broken, their red lettering, saying what is what, half rubbed away. They haven't adjusted the height of the chair to that of the counter so that, at first, from the entrance, you can see only the heads of the people who work there, until you walk right up, stand on your toes, look down to see who he or she is.

Amir doesn't sit behind any counter, he's got a chair of his own and a desk to the left of the entrance, near the main door. His chair is brown moulded plastic, it has iron legs; the desk is made of plywood. It's here that he writes letters for those who can neither read nor write.

His desk is sparse. In one corner, piled high are blank inlands, envelopes, postcards, money order forms. And in the other, a plastic bottle of glue with a piece of cotton wool which he keeps to wipe any stray gum that squeezes out when he seals the envelopes, or drips accidentally from the bottle's brush. There's a candle, too, about three inches high, its molten paraffin frozen hard, clumped at the bottom, a matchbox, a stick of wax, a needle and a thread. The top of the desk is supposed to be horizontal but the wood is old and twisted, the surface has become an incline, making the wax roll down once or twice in a while, so he has propped it up with a low stack of old magazines. He needs the wax because he has to gum and seal the flap of the envelope, sometimes even sew the letter so that it's extra safe. Especially when someone is sending cash.

The post office gets its name from Shimla, a town in the hills almost a thousand miles north by north-west, where the sun is cool during the summer. He has seen posters of this town in the glass windows of the travel agent on Park Street. Title: *Your Switzerland at Home.*

Pictures of Shimla in which cedar trees line the slopes, roads turn into hairpin bends, clouds rest on hills, and in the winter, snow covers the bus stops and the red-tiled roofs of little bungalows with wooden floors. His favourite picture is that of an evening, of a group of people who have lit fires in the snow. He likes the colours – the yellow and the blue of the flames, their reddish tinge, the grey smoke, its purple wisp – all against the white snow, the blue-black of the sky, and the brightly coloured shawls draped over the heads of children who stand close to their parents to keep themselves warm.

Why this post office is called Shimla, he doesn't know.

This morning, Amir is busy. It's the first week of the month so there's a long line at his desk: of handcart-pushers, rickshaw-pullers, carpenters-on-call, masons, maids, all sending a part of their monthly wage to their families back home, far away from the city.

> *My dear, most respected father,*
>   *I hope you are well, with your blessing and*
> *by God's grace, I am well. I am sending you two*
> *hundred and fifty rupees. The family where I work*
> *is a nice family, I work hard and I am eating well.*
> *Sometimes, they give me fruits too. You don't worry*
> *about me. As soon as you get the money, please*
> *show your eyes to the doctor. I hope they don't*
> *water as much. Please give my respects to Mother*
> *and all the elders at home, I will write again next*
> *month, your obedient son.*

It's a perfect fit, the letter ends exactly in the space at the end of the money order form.

It wasn't like this when Amir first started. Every time he would reach the end, the space would run out and the customer would still have two or three paragraphs left. The trick, said Mr Sarkar, the Assistant Postmaster, is to ask them first to tell you what they want to say. Listen to them carefully, then summarize. They don't know how to read so it isn't important which words you use, which words you don't. They have faith in you so cut it down, keep the main points, remove the salutations, I hope you are well, I am well, please convey my regards, I seek your blessings, etcetera, etcetera.

Don't waste space, remember you are sending letters, not writing an essay.

Amir likes Mr Sarkar, especially when he gives advice like this.

Or like this morning when he stops at Amir's desk, on his way to the toilet. Let me tell you, he says, yours may not be a permanent job but it's the best job in the post office, much better than weighing letters, tearing out stamps the whole day. Or putting the seal on registered letters, one by one, until your fingers hurt. They say people now don't use the post office since there are telephones everywhere but let me tell you something, even if they get the most fancy telephones, these poor souls have to send money home and you can't send money through the phone.

And you know what's the next most important thing about your job: honesty. Remember, this is perhaps the only job where you stay clean, where even if you are tempted there's not much you can do, you can't take a bribe to speed up a letter, it will take whatever time it takes, you or I have no control once we drop it into the box. I have heard about crooks in small towns and villages who deliver money only when they keep a bit of it for themselves, but we can't do anything about them. You sit there at your desk and write letters, put the money in the envelopes. Seal, stamp, deliver, that's all. Job done, hands clean.

Get back to work, he says, enough of lecturing for today. I'm an old man who likes to talk.

Mr Sarkar goes back to his desk, begins weighing a huge parcel meant for somewhere in the United States. As the Boss, he gets to handle foreign air mail, weigh aerogrammes.

Amir likes the blue and the red lines drawn along their edges, the small aeroplane, also blue, he likes the sound of the two words on the envelope: *Par Avion*.

One day, he hopes he will send letters that will fly across the ocean.

There's a shadow over his desk, another letter to write. It's a young man, more a boy and he has a lot to say. In fact, so much that Amir stops him midway, says enough, don't tell everything in your first letter, why don't you keep something for the next. The boy smiles, says Sir, please do what you think is best. So he begins writing:

> *Most respected Ma,*
>
> *I am all right, I hope you and Sister are all right as well. I have got a job in a factory where they make shirts meant only for people who live in foreign countries. My job is to pick up each shirt, before it's ironed and packed, check the sleeves, the neck, the bottom, to see whether any thread is sticking out. Most people work from ten to five, but two days in a week, I have to work right through the night, from eight in the evening to five in the morning. Those days I come to work after dinner.*

Don't worry about the food, there are three people
I live with, two of them work in the same factory,
one is a taxi driver. The taxi driver is a nice man,
he will teach me how to drive but for that I need
a ration card. I am trying to get one made. I am
sending you five hundred rupees. Please use two
hundred to repair the wall in the house and then
buy Sister a dress from the market. Please give
Father a glass of milk every day. And, Ma, don't
fast so many days of the week. I hope Sister doesn't
cry.

> *With respects,*
>> *Your son*

The boy hands him the money, five one-hundred rupee notes, and Amir takes out the envelope. This is the part he likes the most since at this stage every customer watches him like a child watching a parent take care of his most precious toy, this is the last time they will get to see their money. So Amir always does this with care, making every effort to ensure that his customers feel safe, reassured. Once again, he counts all the notes, this time aloud, one, two, three, four, five, says five hundred rupees, looks up at the boy who smiles and shakes his head. Amir puts the notes into the envelope, one by one, glues the flap, lights the candle, melts the wax, allows it to drip onto the envelope, takes a tiny seal out of his pocket and presses it hard against the wax.

There, he says, five hundred rupees sealed safe, with your letter, ready to be delivered to your most respected Ma.

The boy, satisfied, turns back and leaves; Amir walks to his desk, looks at his watch.

Why don't you take an early lunch break, says Mr Sarkar, it's been a long day already, come back in an hour, nothing will happen while you are away.

If you are afraid of heights

OR

The afternoon of the accident

IT'S A MAN'S VOICE, it's about half an hour before noon, a crowd has gathered to listen, Amir is there as well. Usually, lunch break is an hour away but today has been a busy day, his hands hurt, he's written letters, counted notes, sealed envelopes, without any break since nine in the morning. Mr Sarkar said why don't you take an early break so he has stepped out and just when he turns the corner, after he has washed the glue off his fingers at a roadside tap, wiped the water against his black trousers, he hears the voice.

'If you are afraid of heights, brothers and sisters, I have nothing to show you, please leave, but if you don't care how high you go, if you don't mind people becoming dots moving up and down the road which becomes a ribbon, then listen to me because I will tell you how you can climb onto my crow's back and fly out of this city.

'Across and over, above and beyond. No pushing in buses, no shoving in trams, no saying sorry, no jumping

puddles of pee, piles of shit. In short, my friends, no headache.

'*And all this thanks to my crow. Look at him, he's in a cage yes, but no, he's not sad, he's at your service, always at your service.*

'*I'll hold him down, don't you worry, just make sure that when you're on top, your legs are firmly pressed against the bird's back, hard and tight. Think it's a horse, you're the rider.*'

It's a man's voice, it's half an hour before noon, a crowd has gathered to listen, about fifty to sixty people, all men who have no need for time.

At a short distance, about four or five feet away, with their backs to this crowd, Amir can see a woman and a child, the woman's hands are dark, her fingers wrinkled, perhaps she's just finished washing the dishes. The child is a girl, eleven to twelve years old, in shirt and a skirt that should have been white, her shirt wrinkled where it was tucked into the skirt and has now come out. Seems the girl's returning home from school. She's pointing to a shop where they have dolls, dressed up. All have golden hair, curled, their faces the colour of sunset, their eyes that of the sky. The little girl is looking at a doll in a red dress with little flowers in front, white and blue, its sleeves with frills made of lace, white and red. The woman, most probably the child's mother, looks tired. She lets herself be dragged by the girl towards the shop window but turns her head in the direction of the voice.

'*Are you scared? There's nothing to be afraid of. Tell me, what's the worst that can happen?*

'*The crow will get angry, he'll fly for just a minute or*

so and then sit on some roof. Well, if that happens, and I'm telling you it won't, cent for cent guarantee, but even if that happens, if the crow lands on someone's roof, just wait for a while. Check if anyone's looking and when you're sure that all's clear, quickly come down the stairs. If they catch you, ask you who you are, where did you come from, why hide the truth? You haven't stolen anything from anybody, just tell them you came down from the sky, on the wings of a crow.'

The crowd laughs, some clap their hands in added appreciation, Amir throws a half-rupee coin, its clink disturbs the crow since it begins to flutter in the cage, its beak sticks out through the bars.

Across the street, they have begun to scrub the floor of the cinema hall lobby. Two boys, both not older than twelve or thirteen, have made mops out of old, torn towels tied at the end of sticks. The woman, with the schoolgirl, can see them, the water in their buckets has turned black. They should throw it, she thinks, refill with fresh water since the dirt is getting back to the floor but then no one's there to check so they don't bother.

And in any case, in half an hour, the noon-show crowd will be here, mainly students bunking classes, some from Church College, some from as far as St Paul's. This show is always an English movie, a title that suggests sex, printed in red letters above a white woman on the poster. This week it's *Indecent Proposal*, crow-droppings streak Demi Moore's neck, someone has torn a bit off Robert Redford's chin.

'I'm sorry, my friends, no heavy men or women allowed, don't get me wrong, my crow is strong, I feed him

well, five times a day, special things, like cream-biscuits, sometimes even chicken and rice, but after all, he's a bird and how much weight can he take?'

The crow flutters, another round of applause, a bus has stopped, some passengers from inside crane their necks to see what's going on, why there's a crowd. Some people walk away to board the bus, new ones join in.

While the girl still admires the doll and her red dress, Amir can see the mother stray towards the crowd, away from the child and towards him.

'Once you've decided, let me know, I'm ready, the crow's ready. We will choose a good time, the best is three or four in the afternoon because that's when the sun is going down, it won't hurt you or the bird. You see, you can wear goggles, my crow can't.'

Another round of laughter, the child has now entered the shop, on her own, the mother's closer to the crowd, listening to each word the man says.

'My crow doesn't need goggles, he's handsome, my black diamond, he's ready to fly. So hop on, sit down, throw your head back, feel the wind in your hair, let him fly.

'In forty to forty-five minutes, one hour maximum, if the wind blows in the right direction, you will reach Chittaranjan Avenue, flying over Bowbazar, its furniture shops, you will be so high you can't smell the turpentine or the varnish.

'And when you are right above the Indian Airlines Building, the crow will take a break there since there's no one on that roof, all are downstairs, working in their offices. Don't wait too long, don't spoil this bird, you've

paid good money, so even if he looks at you with sad eyes, don't give in, get flying again.

'Another half an hour and you'll be over Park Street and Chowringhee, the five-star hotels, maybe if you are lucky, he will take you over the Grand Hotel and you can see people from England, Germany and America.'

Amir's ears take in the voice but his eyes are fixed on the child who is now asking the shopkeeper something. The shopkeeper, a middle-aged man, knows this is a pointless query from a child whose parents cannot pay, so he keeps reading his newspaper, lifts his head twice, nods at the child once, asks her to leave, not waste his time. The child walks out, her eyes lowered to the ground as if she were crying and didn't want anyone to know.

'When you cross Park Street, the scene below will begin to change. The houses will go, their roofs will disappear, so will the children playing there, all gone. Instead of the black tar of the road, the white of the cars, the yellow of the taxis, all you will see will be the green of the Maidan.

'Be careful now since you will soon pass the tallest building in this city, you must have read about it in the papers, heard it on the radio, even seen it on TV, they are all talking about it. It's so tall that my poor crow cannot overfly it, so be careful, the maximum height he can take you to is half of that building.'

The man goes down on his knees and lowers his head to the cage, looks into the crow's eyes, his voice falls; the mother cranes her neck, strains to hear.

'So my dear bird, remember that you have to fly straight, don't look to the left or the right, just slow down

*a bit so that they can see what's inside this building, do
you hear me, are you ready, now?*

'*Silence, total silence, the crow will speak.*'

No one in the crowd moves, all eyes are on the cage,
the child has now come to join her mother and, because
there's a crowd, she stands on her toes so she can see
better. The mother and child are standing next to Amir
now, and a line of people has formed at the cinema's
booking counter.

The crow caws. Once, twice.

'*Yes, yes, brothers and sisters, he's saying yes, yes, he's
ready to take you to Paradise Park, the tallest building in
this city.*

'*Take a ride on my crow and go watch it, not from
the ground, because what will you see from there, nothing,
just another tall building, a building so tall your neck
will hurt. And I hear they are going to build a huge wall
around the building with sharp pieces of glass on it, so
you can't even sneak in at night, but if you're on my
crow's back, there's nothing to worry about, he'll fly you
past, you can look inside and see how they live there.*

'*You could either turn back or keep flying, past Paradise Park, over the new bridge they have built over the
river, past the river, over the factories. Don't worry, hold
tight, my crow will take you higher so that the smoke
from the chimneys doesn't get into your eyes and when
the factories have slipped away beneath you, you will
see the highway like a black ribbon in a girl's hair, down
which you may see a truck or two that take all kinds
of things to villages and to cities like Delhi, Bombay,
Madras.*'

Amir looks at the girl looking at the crow and he sees in her eyes both wonder and excitement. The mother, meanwhile, seems to be fast losing interest as she holds the girl's hand and makes a gesture as if to say let's go now, let's not waste any more time, but the girl looks at her mother with a face to which she cannot say no.

'Then you come to the town where you will see the dirt roads, the small houses, some of brick, some of mud, these days our children don't get to see villages unless they sit by the windows in the railway trains and then, too, they see only the tracks run by at high speed, the houses and the trees rushing past. But my crow doesn't fly that fast, he will let you see everything at your pace.

'And whenever you want to get off, just tell the crow. A tap on his head so that his beak points down and he will know that it's time to stop, he will begin his descent, carefully avoiding the eagles and then land on someone's roof or the ground. Get off and take the bus or the train home, you don't have to worry about the bird, he knows his way back to his cage.'

The crowd is breaking up, many have turned to board the bus that has pulled up at the stop, the mother and the child are gone and Amir looks at his watch, he shouldn't be late at the post office. He turns once to see where the woman and the child have gone but he can't make them out in the crowd on the pavement.

The man has started again: 'If you are afraid of heights, brothers and sisters, I have nothing to show you . . .'

*

When Amir reaches his desk, he cannot concentrate. It's not so much the crow although that does bother him in a way he cannot understand. Waiting for the next customer, he arranges his desk, using his nails to scratch away the crusted gum from the surface, and thinks of the woman and the child he has just seen.

Who could she be?

Maybe she has returned home, he thinks, maybe the child has changed her clothes, had lunch, has begun to cry for the doll in the red dress, her mother has told her to go to sleep, told her when you wake up, you can go and play with the other children and do your schoolwork, I have cleaned the lantern in case there's a power cut. And if you do well in school and if we can save something by then, I'll buy you the doll. The little girl, satisfied, must have gone to sleep leaving her mother alone to wash her face at the roadside hydrant since there would be no water in the bathroom tap.

There are no customers so Amir continues his ride in the train of his thought: while the child sleeps, the mother has to get the housework done, the floors need to be scrubbed, the milk bought. She finishes one room and while she is emptying the black water out of the bucket to refill it for the next, she sees a crow come to rest on the window ledge.

Amir can picture her in his mind as if he were standing by her side: she looks at the bird, imagines herself sitting on its back and smiles at the absurdity of it all. That she, a woman, perhaps thirty or thirty-two, with a child to bring up, the father always gone, always lost in another world, had spent so much time listening to a man tell a stupid story about his crow and the tallest building in this city.

Maybe she begins to feel a little bit guilty as she gets back to work, careful so that her feet don't leave marks on the fresh wet sheen her mop has left on the floor.

Amir wipes his desk clean, scrubs the wax drop that's hardened in one corner. It's time for him to go home.

Mr Sarkar's daughter will be waiting for her evening class.

The evening class

Two sixes are twelve, two sevens are fourteen, two eights are sixteen, two nines are eighteen.

Very good, very good, he says. Now go to the times tables for three and four, right up to ten and then we'll go to the English lesson.

Amir is in the kitchen where he's chopping onions for dinner. The potatoes have been boiled, to his left is the turmeric powder, a pinch kept ready in a teaspoon.

I want to hear you from here, he says, I don't want to hear any pauses, no gaps, otherwise you have to repeat the whole thing, from two to ten.

The girl obeys.

She's here five days a week and the sequence is the same; they start with arithmetic, then he helps her with her school homework and they wrap up with an English lesson. For her homework today, she has to draw a teacup and paint it using tube colours. Amir's not good at these things so he tells her to draw it on her own, and she doesn't ask him for help. She sits there, on his floor, and with a pencil, she draws a teacup, begins to colour it yellow, the tea brown, adds the wisp of smoke rising from the surface.

Today's English lesson is from a book called *Learning English,* from a chapter called 'Robert Bruce', the brave king who took shelter in a cave in a far-off land after his enemies drove him away from the kingdom.

'In the cave, he noticed a spider trying to make a cobweb on the ceiling. The stone walls of the cave were uneven and the spider kept slipping down but every time it did, at once it started to climb the wall again, holding the thread in its feet.

'Then it nearly reached the top but then, alas! It landed on the same spot from where it started.

'The king observed the spider's sad and difficult condition. He compared his fate with that of the spider. He also tried to rescue his kingdom many times but he failed. Should he then hide in a cave like a coward? Never!'

Amir reads slowly, she listens, looks at the page, at his finger which moves from one word to the other.

'The spider started to climb again. Once again, it had a fall. It fell seven times but did not give up. It tried again and this time it succeeded in reaching the top. The king learnt a lesson from the spider.'

His eyes move away to see the hair falling over her ears, she brushes it aside, he notices the way she tucks it behind her little ear, he can see her nails, tiny and pink. He is careful, he never scolds her, once he had raised his voice and she had begun to cry.

The oil crackles in the kitchen.

Give me five minutes, he says, why don't you think of the answers to the first three questions at the end of the lesson.

Why did Robert Bruce take shelter in a cave?

What was the spider trying to make?

Did the spider give up hope?

He stirs the potatoes to spread the turmeric evenly, the rice he will cook when he's back at night. He covers the potatoes one last time, he likes the noise the frying makes through the lid, like the rain on a tin roof.

She is touching up the teacup she has drawn, adding a handle, a question mark. Her fingers aren't steady, the line wavers, a bit of the handle enters the cup where the tea is and she looks up at him, smiles, looks down again, uses the eraser to rub away the offending curve.

Have you got the answers, he asks.

She nods her head, without looking up from the drawing book.

Did the spider give up hope? he asks.

No, she says, it did not have any, so how could he give it up.

Don't write that, he says, just write that the spider didn't give up hope, he kept climbing back trying to reach the top.

She nods again, begins collecting her things from the floor, her pencil box, the exercise book, the two books she brought, arithmetic and English. She knows it's time to leave. Amir feels guilty, not much work got done today, but he'll make up for it the next time. He leads her to the door and watches her turn the latch, her little finger, smooth, no wrinkles on her knuckles as they brush against his ugly door.

Hold the railing and then walk down the stairs slowly, he says, it's dark.

It's six-thirty, time for him to leave for Park Street, the potatoes are done, he pierces them with his spoon to check. He returns to his room and while he's sitting in the chair, putting on his shoes, he can see the grey flecks on the floor which she has left behind in his house, the scattered remains of the line she drew and then erased. He lets them be.

It's less than six hours before the accident and so far it's been, except for the silly incident with the man and the crow, just another ordinary day in his ordinary life.

It's all going to change but that's still hours away as he walks down the stairs, past the cobbler who is preparing to leave for the day, the sweet shop where the children are wiping the tables, across the street to the bus stop. On his way to Park Street.

Park Street

OR

The evening of the accident

AROUND SEVEN in the evening is when Amir reaches
Park Street, when all the stores have switched their lights
on except the small, makeshift stalls on the pavement,
made of only benches and tents, which sell imported cigarettes and gas lighters, sugarfree gum, Swiss Army knives,
soap from China, condoms from Japan, which have nude
women on their shiny covers, their hair orange, their
breasts bigger than their heads. These stalls don't do much
business because people suspect they sell fakes, so except
for newcomers to the city, from villages or small towns,
no one stops here, not even to look.

The result: their owners don't have enough money to
buy lightbulbs of their own and that's why, although it's
illegal, each one of them pays fifty rupees every day to the
local policeman who, in turn, lets them set their stalls right
in front of the big shops so that they can share the light.

*

Amir's walk begins from where these stalls start on Park Street, off the main road. He gets off the bus and stands for a while in front of the Asiatic Society, a squat, red-brick building with a brass plaque near its entrance: *An institute of national importance, dedicated to research and scholarship in history, founded by Sir William Jones.*

Next to this plaque is a blue board with white letters saying *Stick No Bills* but no one seems to have read it and Amir's attention is drawn to the posters pasted right and left, above and below. He likes reading them slowly, word by word.

Join Academy of Higher Education, Don't Miss the Computer Bus, Learn Data Entry, Java, HTML. One day he will enrol, he tells himself, everyone at the post office says these days you need to know what a computer is otherwise soon you will be out of a job.

Fifth Week Running, House Full, Globe Cinema, Matinee, Evening, Night, Indecent Proposal. There are two foreign actors, a man and a woman, and although he doesn't know who these people are – he has never seen an English movie before – he likes the way the woman looks at him, her strong chin, her short black hair, her bare arms.

Around this poster are more handbills: *Sengupta & Sons Electrics, Call for Inverters.*

Madonna Clips Beauty Parlour, Coming Soon to the Maidan.

Nailed onto a banyan tree, at eye level, is a white aluminium board: *Marie Stopes Clinic, No Questions Asked, Rs 400, Walk in, walk out after half an hour.* The

tree is old, its topmost branches almost touch the tram-
wires above the street.

Two dozen steps and he's reached 'Readers' Heaven'
where the shop window looks like a bus stop for books,
crowded with titles of all kinds, some sitting, most
standing, all staring out at the street. His eyes first stop at
the large ones, those with glossy pictures on their covers.
Of things he hasn't seen, except on TV at the Shah's kiosk
and sometimes in his dreams: a stream flowing down a
cliff; cedar trees lining the road; people in parachutes
against the sky; birds he has never seen even at the zoo,
with blue beaks and red tails, birds as big as dogs; tall
buildings in cities far away, across the seven seas, buildings
that lean into each other leaving just a narrow strip of the
sky through which their shadows fall on the street below.
Then there are books wrapped in transparent plastic, their
covers teasing him with pictures of women, nude, not the
entire woman but only a bare leg or an arm, the curve of
the back, the neck. Sometimes only the face.

He walks into the store, there are people in the aisle,
men and women, their eyes fixed on the spines of the
books on the shelves, not looking down where their feet
move slowly, step by step. Besides the books, he likes to
look at the stationery, especially the new glue tubes, those
should help at the post office, no need to use that brush
any more, that ugly bottle, and get gum on your fingers
which then dries and you have to scrape it off with a lot
of soap and water.

The tube isn't all that expensive, fifteen rupees compared with the ten for the glue pot he uses. He decides to
speak to Mr Sarkar one of these days, ask him to make

the change in the Materials Acquisition Form so that after the current stock of gum is over they can switch to the tube, a little bit more expensive but so much more efficient.

Past the bookshop, there is a lane that veers off the street and at its end, through a large, iron gate, Amir can see a cluster of houses, women standing on the balconies, leaning on the rails, maybe waiting for their husbands to return late from the office. Amir stops to watch.

Children play with the iron gate, climbing onto its base, adjusting their feet between the bars, telling the guard to keep pushing the gate, opening and closing it, opening and closing, like a swing, the sound of their laughs mixing with the creak of the gate. One child, a little girl, jumps off the gate, looks at her palms, at the marks which the bars have left, makes a face, brushes them against her dress, climbs back.

What do you need, the guard asks Amir. Looking for anyone?

No, nothing, I just stopped for a while.

Move ahead, there's nothing to see here, this is private.

Another man, perhaps the guard's attendant, appears from behind the gate.

Want to see something, go down the street and look at Park Hotel, he says. They both laugh.

Amir walks on, he can hear a child crying, perhaps it slipped off the gate, bruised a knee.

His next stop is the auction house.

It has mostly things from fifty to one hundred years

ago: wooden beds with iron posts, mirrors so big they can only be used in movies, smaller things as well. Like a ship's compass he can't understand, a telescope, ceramic birds taking off from ceramic trees, their wings and beaks caught in mid-air, their tails inlaid with glass flowers, blue, white and red. Tiny marble replicas of the Victoria Memorial in a glass box, complete with a fake landscape of the green Maidan, the banyan trees in miniature. Even a tiny wooden ice-cream cart with a tiny man made of blackened metal.

He steps inside, he likes the smell of old wood, turpentine and polish. The interior is a sprawling hall, lit only by four electric bulbs, not more than a hundred watts each. Most of the items there are wrapped in their shadows. Nothing is arranged in any order but the two attendants have taken care to ensure that there is a little passageway between the piles of goods so that you can walk in and around without bumping into the furniture or grazing against the glass.

Do you need anything? The man in charge walks up to him, an old man in glasses, who walks with a limp.

Just looking, says Amir.

This isn't a museum you know, the man mutters, irritated, under his breath. Let me know if you want to buy something.

There's no one else in the shop, Amir can't understand why in a city so crowded he's the only one here, where there's so much to look at.

How much is this lamp, he asks. It has a brass stand and a shade made of stained glass.

Five hundred rupees, the man says, and watches Amir walk out of the shop.

These people don't have anything to do, only waste their time, says the man, making sure that Amir hears each word.

For the next week or so, Amir tells himself, he will avoid that shop: he will be careful, he will walk past, maybe slow down to look but will never enter unless he's sure that there's a different attendant in the shop.

It's well past eight, the late evening crowd is flowing in as if someone has opened the sluices to an invisible gate where the better-dressed had stood waiting right through the day for the street to clean itself up. Taxis and cars begin to pull up, one by one, in front of restaurants, people get off, tell their drivers to wait as they walk in groups, confident and assured, welcomed at the gate by waiters dressed in black and white. One or two of the guests, usually men, break away to buy cigarettes or matchboxes and then rejoin the women who hang on to their children staring at the beggars crawling down the street, one man with nothing below his waist, one woman with her child fast asleep over one arm, the other extended for some change.

By now, Amir has reached Park Hotel, the end of the street, it's time to wind up the walk, return. His feet hurt, he stands in the arcade, he likes looking at the flower bed in the driveway that leads to the hotel's lobby, at the hibiscus and the jasmine, a palm and several roses. And when no one is looking, he bends down, plucks one, puts it in his shirt pocket, carefully, so that its petals don't get crushed.

The guard at the hotel is dressed up like in story books, with a turban made of shimmering satin, its pleats red and yellow, leather slippers with hand-painted designs that curve in a curl at the tip. Amir can feel the guard looking right through him, at some point on the road where another car has pulled up, its doors open, rich feet step out in shoes, beautiful and polished, the street light bouncing off the leather. Amir looks down, sees his own shoes streaked with mud. He must give them to the cobbler tomorrow, ask him to use some extra cream.

He turns left on Free School Street where the prostitute lives. This is his last stop before the accident tonight.

The prostitute

OR

Hours before the accident

THE PROSTITUTE'S ROOM on Free School Street is on the first floor of a two-storey house, the ground floor of which is a studio called 'Flash Express' with a white cloth banner strung across the entrance saying *Passport Photos in Five Minutes, Frames That Will Last You a Life*. The shop window is a small glass cupboard in which they have six pictures, two of young men in suits, two of women with bobbed hair, one must be of a newly wed couple, since the bride has a lot of jewellery around her neck, and the last one of a baby fast asleep in a pram in a park. They haven't changed these pictures in months and Amir knows them by heart, the exact sequence, the way they have been thumbtacked onto a board, in two parallel rows of two, the picture of the couple above, that of the baby below.

The man in charge of the studio knows what happens upstairs but doesn't mind.

*

Amir knocks and she opens the door. The room is much smaller than his – he notices this every time he comes here – eight feet by eight feet, approximately; there's an attached toilet, its door slightly ajar, she always keeps it this way so that standing in the middle of the room he can see one corner of the sink inside. The walls are yellow, half-draped in shadows by a single light bulb which hangs from the ceiling by a cord.

The bulb's not milky, it's plain glass in which he can see the filament, it hurts his eyes. Just below the light bulb is the double bed against the window, the headboard inches away from the wall, two pillows propped against it, shaped like hearts, all covered with a white bedsheet, like in hotels. On the window sill, there's a small dog made of ceramic, brown with white patches on its neck, its tail chipped off into a stump. Perhaps, it fell off the sill during a strong wind when the window was open.

The window has a wooden frame painted green but its pane is missing: where there should be glass are pasted pages from newspapers, one English, the other Bengali. There's a tear in the paper through which light from the street outside can squeeze itself in.

The last time he was here was a week ago. Mr Sarkar's daughter had skipped her evening class making him leave home early. He had reached here before evening, even before sunset, so that when she sat down on the bed, he had seen the red afternoon light stream in through the tear in the paper-pane, light the dust specks as they danced on their own before dancing down to the bed, brushing her shoulder.

This evening, however, all he can see is a black slit of

the darkness outside. And hears only the shuffle of feet from maybe a customer who's come to have his or her picture taken below.

She doesn't say a word, turns her back to him, begins to undress.

Standing, he watches her clothes fall onto the floor, one by one. The sari is a big red and yellow heap, it reminds him of flowers, wet and used, marigold and hibiscus, piled high outside the Kalighat temple. One of these days, he thinks, he's going to surprise her by buying a sari more soft and subtle, maybe white and sky blue, like the ones he sees models wearing in magazines. Maybe during Durga Puja.

She unbuttons her blouse, slips it over her head, it rumples her hair; the bra is the next to go, he can see where its white straps have gouged themselves on her brown back. The petticoat's tied with a string she pulls and then lets drop. Then she turns to him, naked and smiling.

Why do you do this every time? she asks. No one does this, watch me undress. Go take everything off, I won't look.

She turns her back, he can see her red welts, the fat on the sides, her thighs streaked with stretch marks, there's a mole on her right buttock, her nipples so dark they look like shadows, there's a bruise on one.

As she lies on the bed, adjusting herself so that her head settles snugly against the pillow, he moves away. Turning his back to her, he undresses, and folds his trousers over the chair so that the pleats remain. He paid three rupees for the ironing, they need to last him one more day.

She closes her eyes as she holds him, strokes him until he's hard. She turns her head, slightly to her left, to bring out the condom from underneath the pillow, uses her teeth and her fingers to tear the plastic wrap.

He moves inside her, his face inches above hers, she moves, her hair brushes against his eyes, he brushes it away, he can see yesterday's newspaper stuck to the window frame, *Girl Found Dead in Small Town,* he reads. He can smell the talcum powder on her neck, the whiff of oil in her hair, the sheen of sweat on her forehead. He can hear someone laughing from the street outside, a child crying, a mother telling her to go to bed.

He knows he's about to come, he delays it by shutting his eyes and opening the door inside his head to let the cockroaches come crawling out, the buckets full and heavy go up the stairs, the spider on the wall watched by Robert Bruce, the glue at the post office wrinkle his fingers.

They are both lying in bed, she on her side, facing the wall, he facing her back. He likes this part the best, when they are close it reminds him of a pair of inverted commas on a blank sheet of paper.

Sleepy? she asks.

A bit, he says.

You have three hours, do what you want to do.

She moves to make herself more comfortable but doesn't change her position. His elbows cast shadows on her back.

How long will you keep coming here, she asks, why don't you get married?

Because she's facing the wall and because she's speaking softly, he can't hear all the words but he understands.

How do you know I am not married? he says.

Oh, yes, you may be, with a wife and a child but you want me to find a nice girl for you? The man downstairs, who runs the studio, has a daughter who goes to college. Just the right age, well, a little young but girls these days grow up fast.

She laughs without making a noise. He can see the ridge on her back that rises and falls, he snuggles close, likes the touch of her warm skin against his, brown against brown, the back of her thighs against his legs.

Ten minutes pass, she is silent, she must have fallen asleep and to check, he slowly moves his left hand across and over her back, he can see its shadow move on the wall. He brings his fingers close to her face and gently brushes them against her right eye, he traces its curve, can't feel the eyelids flutter.

He lets his hand stay that way, it's awkward, but that's the closest he can get to hugging her and although he feels nothing special for her, he likes doing this, likes counting her eyelashes.

They both fall asleep, the lamp still glowing, bathing them with its harsh yellow.

It's half an hour before midnight when she wakes him up, her night shift is going to begin.

Before putting his trousers on, he takes the wallet out of the back pocket, and pays her, standing there in the middle of the room, water streaking his leg where he has washed. She counts ten five-rupee notes, he pays her twenty rupees extra and for that she lets him help her with the sari, hold its folds down on the floor while she adjusts her border. She even lets him button up her blouse. And then she watches him dress, brushes away a piece of lint stuck in his hair. The flower he picked up at the hotel this evening falls out of his shirt's pocket.

You keep it, he says.

See you next week, she says.

He's out, back on the street, feeling the wetness in his trousers, the dull ache. The studio is now closed, its shutters down. They are plastered with posters of films long gone.

Amir turns right, back onto Park Street which is now slowly slipping into the shadows, only a couple of restaurants are open. Through the glass windows he can see the last of the customers at a few tables, the waiters busy wiping the others. In one, they have already stacked the chairs on the tables, upside down. He can't understand why they do this, maybe this helps them scrub the floor.

He walks fast, the last tram leaves at midnight, in five more minutes. A light wind has begun to blow, it's the night wind from across the river. He passes the book shop, they don't remove the books from the window, just lower a huge iron gate with bars, like the gate in a prison cell, he has always wondered how easy it is to break in, push a rod between the bars, smash the window, steal a book.

When he reaches the end of Park Street, he can see, across the road, the terminus, hear the clanging of the trams as they retire for the night, the whine of their wheels.

He boards the tram. It's empty, so he walks to his favourite seat, right in front, just behind the driver's cabin. The driver hasn't shown up yet, he will board in a few minutes so Amir begins reading the poster in the tramcar: a large white rectangle, a sheet of paper in a glass and wooden frame with tiny lettering. He's read it so many times that he almost knows it by heart but he reads it once again: *The first horse-drawn tramcar service was introduced in New York, USA, in November 1832. At New Orleans, a 4 mile long Tramway services opened in 1835, is still operating as the world's oldest tramways.* The punctuation is in the wrong places, the grammar is wrong, 4 mile long should be hyphenated, Amir wants to correct it. *In Europe, regular tram services were introduced for the first time in Paris in 1855 and then in Versailles in 1856. Berlin and Vienna had tramway services since 1865, Moscow in 1874.*

In India, the first tram service was inaugurated in this city in 1873, with a procession of three tramcars, each being pulled by two Australian horses. The existing electrics dates back to 1900. Exactly one hundred years ago, Amir says to himself.

The tram has begun to move, he sees the back of the driver, his brown uniform, his feet on the pedal as he turns the crank and the tram pulls out, on its way towards the Maidan which through the window is a sea of black. But Amir's eyes, as of now, are still on the poster, on the last line: *We carry about 5.5 lakh passengers every day to their destinations.*

It's moments before the accident.

The accident

Next morning, this is how *The Newspaper* reports the accident on page three, in double column, with a headline in two lines. It's the most objective account there is of the circumstances in which Rima and Amir first met.

TWO TRAMS COLLIDE IN FREAK ACCIDENT

By a Staff Reporter

THE CITY: In what experts say is the first accident of its kind in this city, two trams collided head-on last night. Because of the late hour, both trams were, in all likelihood, empty. No casualties have been reported so far.

The two drivers were injured and, according to the Medical Superintendent at the City Post Graduate hospital, both are out of danger.

The accident occurred minutes after one in the morning when the No 14 tram, after completing its half-a-mile loop around the Maidan, had crossed Paradise Park and pulled into Esplanade while on the parallel line, the No 26 from the Railway Station was minutes away from its terminus.

'One of them must have derailed,' said a Tramways official who did not want to be named.

'And it was a coincidence that the other tram was there exactly at the same time. Such a coincidence hasn't happened in living memory. We will, of course, inquire into what exactly went wrong.'

There are 405 trams which carry 600,000 passengers every day in the city on 29 routes.

Sources said that both drivers had twenty years of experience each and it was unlikely that the trams derailed at the same time. However, the possibility of faulty brakes isn't being ruled out.

Among the eyewitnesses was a man who was turning in for the night at the bus-stop shelter.

'Barely had I closed my eyes when I heard the sound of metal colliding with metal, a ringing and then glass breaking . . . at first, I thought a truck had crashed against a lamp post or a house had come down but when I opened my eyes, I saw the trams, both off their tracks . . . I couldn't even recognize the drivers' cabins.'

According to some local residents who rushed to the site minutes after the accident, there were two passengers, a man and a woman, but whether they were travelling in the same tram wasn't clear.

'She helped the man get up but when we offered to help, she declined saying that she lived just around the corner,' said a middle-aged man who was the first to go to the local police station and get an ambulance for the drivers.

'The man had blood on his face but could walk, helped by the woman.'

However, no official confirmation was available of whether there were any passengers.

Sources said that the drivers would be interrogated once their condition was 'stable'.

Incidentally, the technology used by the Tramways Corporation has changed little from what it was when the first electrified service began in 1902.

Even the design of the trolley bars that provide power from the overhead wires is still the same.

In fact, while elsewhere in the world, tracks and wires are being improved and refined to increase speeds, trams in this city are trundling from bad to worse.

When contacted, Mr D. K. Dasgupta, Managing Director of the Tramways Corporation, declined to comment and added that he had ordered a departmental inquiry.

Waking up in Paradise Park

WAKING UP IN Rima's room in Paradise Park, the first thing Amir sees is a pale white light, the first thing Amir feels is a cool draft against his body. He's been sleeping for over five hours. More like adrift for over five hours on waves of pain that begin from between his eyes, grow as they travel down his back to his feet and then up, over his knees, his waist, chest, neck before crashing against his eyes again. He is wrapped in a medicinal haze of ointments, gels that drench the cotton gauze tied firmly around his head. When he opens his eyes, it takes him a moment to realize that the pale white light is not light from a special bulb, covered with a special filter. This is light from the sky, the first light of day. It floods the room, filling every space available. It softens the edges of the brown table in front, even lights his nails and his hands, gets brighter and brighter before his eyes.

In this light, he looks around, moves his head, just a little bit, the pain making him wince. Where is the light coming from?

Through the narrow strip of glass on the wall opposite his bed.

But, no, this is neither a strip of light nor a rectangular shaft, it's a flood that pours forth from the wall as if the wall itself had turned luminescent. For this time Amir's eyes have adjusted and he can see that the wall is made of glass and the light is filtering through curtains. The cool draft against his face? Is it a fan? There's no fan on the ceiling, only a chandelier, a huge glass plant hanging upside down with flowers and leaves, several ceramic birds resting on its stalks, their beaks and wings caught in mid-air, each holding a light bulb.

There's no stand-fan on the floor anywhere but the draft is strong enough to make the ends of his sheet quiver. Maybe some door is open, some door he cannot see and the wind is rushing through it. He thinks of other options and then he hears it, the hum, so light that he would have missed it had it not been for the silence in the room. It's an air conditioner. He has seen one in the Bombay Dyeing store – near the cinema hall, just around the corner from the post office – where he once went to buy a towel but didn't since everything was so expensive and yet they didn't mind him looking around, staying inside for a while, without buying, just to dry his sweat before stepping into the furnace outside. That was cold and harsh, there were six or seven air conditioners, all lined up on one side of the wall, looking like giant machines in some ice factory, but this draft is cool, much more gentle. Like the wind carrying the first drops of rain, when the monsoon breaks, when the heat suddenly vanishes as if a giant switch has been flicked off in the sky, drawing thick, black clouds over the sun.

The light and the draft explained, Amir's attention turns to where he lies. The sheet that covers him is white, and smells of soap, fresh water. The bed is so big he could roll over three times and still not fall but he can't move now, his back is stiff. He can feel a weight on his chest so heavy that even the slightest shift and he feels a knife in his back. Someone twisting it, bit by bit. He's dressed in a white loose-fitting robe, a gown, a little like what the barber puts around his neck when he goes for a haircut but this isn't plastic, it's a kind of fabric that snuggles against his body, warm and white. Under the gown, he can see, he is naked.

He turns on one side to see a green carpet covering the floor like water in a pond, mixed with mud and earth. The carpet runs underneath the table in the corner, right up to the wall, almost touching the curtains, under the bed, behind the door, which is slightly ajar and through which he can see only a strip of grey wall that perhaps leads to the other rooms.

In one of which Rima lies, maybe still fast asleep.

He lets his hand fall, it hurts, but fortunately he doesn't have to bend or stretch, the bed's height seems to be perfect since his fingers touch the carpet. He runs them through the fine fibres, moves them left right, left right, wipers on a wet windshield, the green changes into light green, dark green, light green again. Like the surface of a paddy field when the stalks move this way and that in a strong wind.

His eyes close. It's brighter in the room now, the light seeps through his closed eyes, tinting the darkness with a heavy daub of grey. Before the second wave of sleep crashes against the shores of his eyes, scraps from last night and last morning float by: the clang of the buckets, the gurgle of the tap, the letters at the post office, the tram window he was looking out of, its wooden frame shuddering, cold to his head, the gibberish so elegantly framed that he knows it almost by heart, the dates, 1832 and 1873, the fact that the first trams in the city were drawn by horses.

At first these images appear in an orderly sequence, as if he were standing on some balcony looking out at a parade, but soon they start getting mixed up, breaking and joining only to break again. He sees the horses trot up his stairs with the buckets slung around their necks, their manes soaked and shining in the rain, a letter he wrote at the post office framed in the tram, people reading and laughing, Mr Sarkar's daughter fast asleep in the turret of the tank in the Maidan, Bomba crying and then smiling as he hands him the stamps, Rima standing in line waiting for him to write her letter, a man flying on a crow's back.

And then there is sleep again.

The next few days pass by

THE NEXT FEW DAYS pass by in a blur slowing down
once in a while before picking up speed again like a dust
storm before the rain that sends everything into a spin,
erases boundaries, blunts edges, blows grit into your eyes,
whips the edges of your dress, claps shreds of paper against
the ankles and then makes them float down, get trapped
in some nook or angle of your shoe. That's how each day
whirls past Amir mixing objects with events, words with
sounds, smells with tastes. While he himself, in sharp
contrast, lies still most of the time.

Getting up once in a while to walk to the window,
from the window to the wall and back to the bed. Sometimes Rima enters the room but only to sit beside the bed
in a chair, then get up and leave.

You don't have to talk now, she says, let's wait until
you get better.

What strikes him first, between his half-closed eyes, on his
hands, below his feet, with an impact that sometimes
seems to him stronger than that of the accident, is the new
world he finds himself in. All its glitter and all its gleam.
He doesn't try to resist, instead he suspends all that he

knows so that to an observer, looking in through the door, this grown-up man seems like a child, walking around in a shop containing all the things in the world, both imagined and unimagined.

This begins right from the time he wakes up in the morning to the pale light from the window and the draft from the air conditioner. Every movement makes him aware of a detail, new and fascinating, and whenever he repeats that movement, the detail comes back to him. As if he were seeing it for the very first time.

Beginning with the carpet, its green fibres tickle his toes, like grass, fresh and dry, then the bathroom, the coloured tiles on the floor, the fittings and the faucets. He turns them on, watches the water flow out, cold and warm, the sink white without a single speck anywhere, the bathtub resting on four brass legs, shaped like tigers' paws, its nails made of some material like alabaster that sparkles in the invisible lights sunk into the ceiling which wrap the gleam in the bathroom with a glow the like of which he has never seen before.

Once in a while, like breath against a mirror on a winter's day, Amir can see the past take a formless shape. He can see his own cold red cement floor, cracked; his taps dry, the toilet bowl stained in several places. But as the days pass by, one after the other, so do these images until he learns how to adjust the faucets in the bathtub to get the right mix of water, hot and cold; he learns how to use the toilet bowl sitting so that his feet rest on the floor.

*

Breakfast, lunch and dinner, all three times Rima brings the food and keeps it on a steel table, with a circular top, beside his bed. The dishes are made of china in which he can see finely carved drawings of people dancing, holding hands, all in stick figures. He can't name any of the things on the plate but bits and pieces look familiar, slices of potatoes, eggs, a piece of chicken. He can make out the grains of rice but these are much longer, finer than he's ever had or seen.

Afternoons, he wakes up when the doctors come, two of them. One is perhaps an assistant since he always follows the other, carries his briefcase, passes him whatever he wants, stands while the other sits on the bed and feels Amir's forehead. He likes the smell of the soap on the doctor's hands, the hair on his wrists brushing his face.

The doctor peels off the bandage so gently that Amir can't even feel it except for a sudden coolness when it's off, when the air fans his healing wounds and when the doctor, with a piece of cotton wool drenched in antiseptic liquid, wipes the crusted ointment away.

The pain, which at first came in stabs, as if a knife were being scraped against his forehead, has now reduced to a dull ache, more like a headache in the heat, the kind he often has at the end of a long powerless night in the summer. The doctor gets up, lets the assistant apply the ointment afresh with a cotton swab and then the dressing, a white cotton gauze that he wraps around his forehead several times before fixing it in place at the back of his head, with a pair of clips.

All the while, Amir lies still, his eyes closed but half awake to the smell of medicine, listening to the scraps of conversation that float around in the room, between the doctor and his assistant. And sometimes with Rima who must have entered quietly and is standing by the door watching.

How much longer do you think? she asks.

We can't take any chances, he's getting along fine but let's keep changing the dressing, applying the ointment, the doctor says.

The wound just missed his eyes, says the assistant. He is lucky.

Is he hurting? she asks.

I think so, says the doctor, but we have given medicines to numb the pain, to help him fall asleep.

Thank you, she says, I am glad you aren't taking any chances.

The dressing done, the assistant puts a hand under Amir's head and helps him get up for the pills. Eyes closed, he swallows them with water, cold and sparkling, from a plastic cup filled by the assistant from a purple glass pitcher which sits on the bedside table.

You sleep now, Rima says.

He can hear the assistant snap the briefcase shut and, with the doctor, walk out of the room, their steps receding. When you get up, dinner will be on the table by your bed, she says. He turns to thank her but she stops him: You don't have to talk now, she says, let's wait until you get better.

The pills work. From the moment Rima leaves with the doctors, Amir slides into a sleep that pulls him right through the evening and well into the night when he wakes up, drained.

Dinner helps. The plate is warm. He pulls the table to the bed and eats, rinses his mouth with a glass of water and goes back to sleep again. Unlike the first night, when images from his past haunted his sleep, hammering against his closed eyelids, now it's more uneventful. Perhaps it's the medicine, perhaps it's the pain, Amir isn't sure but he realizes he sleeps more soundly now, not even turning during the night. In fact, when he wakes up in the morning, he finds that the sheet he pulled over himself in the night is still spread straight, there are only a few wrinkles here and there, some above his knee and where his toes are. The pillow isn't turned or twisted, not a single crease in its white case.

Sleep and waking and sleep again, eating in between. So simple is this routine that Amir soon settles in and it's a matter of days and nights before he begins getting accustomed to the objects around him, the same objects that, a short while ago, so strongly held his fascination.

Until one morning when Amir discovers the view from the window.

The view from the window

LATER, HE WILL WONDER how he missed this at first. Because wasn't this the first thing he noticed when he woke up in Paradise Park? Wasn't this the same window through which he saw the pale light flood his room? So many times he walked up and down the room, treading softly across the carpet to the window, so many times he stopped there and yet how did it slip his attention?

These questions don't matter this morning as he stands near the window. And looks out.

Both instinct and common sense tell him he should see the street below and because he's standing high up, higher than he has ever been, everything should appear smaller: the trucks like cars, the roads like lanes, the people like children. But this isn't what he sees. Instead, the sky both above and below, stretching in front, in bands of colour, white and blue, static at first and then bending, mixing, into yellow and red. And nothing else.

He lowers his eyes, the same endless expanse, not even the faintest sign, the vaguest blur of green or brown or black of the earth below to break the whiteness of the sky.

Although his feet are firmly on the carpet and he can feel its now familiar rough-smooth texture, he feels he's suspended in mid-air, or flying, then plummeting down into a sea, sluggish and heavy, into which he splashes without a sound, begins to drown, the water filling his mouth, his lungs, his entire body.

He stumbles, his head reeling.

He holds the edge of the chair to steady himself and closes his eyes, hoping that by doing so he can shut out the distortion that has suddenly, blindingly overwhelmed his world. He opens his eyes and, with his back to the window, walks to the bed to lie down amid the more familiar shapes. Pillows, the flat surface of the sheet, the reassuring rustle of their fabric against his skin, the hard, reliable edges of his bed.

I'm being stupid, he tells himself, thank God no one's in the room, I'm worse than a child, let me try again.

This time he approaches the window cautiously, his eyes averted from the glass as he stands a few feet away, looks first at his feet on the floor, the nails on his toes, feels confident that nothing will slip from underneath him, and then moves his eyes upwards, stopping to watch the window's frame, solid, rectangular, brown and wooden. No, there's nothing to be afraid of, he tells himself, whatever I saw is what lies outside, it's safely shut out.

I need to tilt the glass, Rima says.

She's standing at the door, smiling, like a mother watching someone else's child take the first few steps. She's leaning, as if she had been standing there for a while, looking at him.

Everyone makes this mistake the first time, she says, don't worry.

She walks to the window, and as she passes him, he can smell the shampoo in her hair that falls to her shoulders in one smooth wave. She bends down and presses what looks like a switch on a panel below the window. This makes the glass tilt outward, noiselessly and slowly, a fraction of an inch a second until it comes to stop at an angle to the ground. And as it moves, Amir can see the sky move with it as well and what was just white and blue is beginning to stain brown and green as the glass, now inclined downwards, catches the ground and the grass below.

There it is, can you see it now? Rima says. That's the Maidan.

Amir should be wonderstruck but what overshadows the awe is the sense of comfort that the sight of the Maidan brings, the assurance that the ground beneath his feet which had moved just moments ago has slid back into its familiar place.

Now through the glass, he can see the Maidan like an enormous blanket, green and discoloured in several places, spread out to dry on the ground, the trees like tiny clumps of leaves that have dropped onto it.

Can you see the little dots, each moving at its own speed, Rima says, those are people. Look how the dots are scattered in the middle, she says, in ones and twos, but as you move towards the edges where the road is, where the tramlines are, you can see them bunched together, like bubbles in the water at the mouth of a drain.

I like watching them, she says, especially when two or three dots move together, you know they are friends out for a walk.

Or when one dot breaks free from a bunch, darts a

little distance in front, darts back, you know that's a child. You see more of that in the evening while now, in the morning and in the afternoon, the dots cluster at the edges waiting for a tram or a bus.

As he listens to her, Amir's eyes travel beyond what she's saying, searching the landscape that has suddenly unfolded in front for landmarks and scenes that he's familiar with. There's a thin dark line, staggered, blotched, maybe this is Park Street, the black could be the tar being freshly laid but from this height he cannot be sure since he can't make out any of the stores he knows so well. He looks across the Maidan to identify the old Russian tank, it must be somewhere to the right. He sees a speck that doesn't move, larger than a dot, smaller than a cluster, maybe that's the one but then there's no evidence of the barbed wire fence around it, no line ringing the speck.

What he can see clearly are the advertising billboards on the road. He can make out some of the large letters, not clearly enough to read a word or a sentence. He can see the water tanks atop the Grand Hotel, tiny grey boxes of concrete, with pipes coming in and going out, a wisp of steam rising from one roof.

Where is your house? Rima asks. Can you point it out to me?

It's south of Park Street, so it should be straight ahead and then to the right, but when Amir looks, all he can see is roof after roof, the tops of houses, like newspaper pictures of villages after a flood, aerial views of the damage and the debris. And yet in this jumble, there's some kind of an order, the roofs all rectangular, each of a distinct length and breadth, the cityscape laid out like a radio set opened inside out.

His mind tries to recall landmarks while his eyes search for something, anything that stands out in this ocean of concrete. He remembers a water tank not far from where his house is but now he can see several, scattered all around. His landlord had planted a flag on the roof once upon a time but he sees no coloured speck, maybe it was taken down. There's a park near his house but it's too small to show up.

So without saying anything, he points his fingers in the direction, south. It should be somewhere there, he says.

Rima doesn't press for any details.

Can you tilt the window any other way? he asks.

Yes, she says, that's why on certain nights when the sky is clear, when the Maidan is dark, when the wind has blown away the dust and the smoke, you can see the sea, which is five hundred miles away, right in front.

You can see the waves, Rima says, the foam and the spray crashing against the shore, the crabs trying to hold on to the sand, the gulls flying, and because sound cannot be telescoped, the whole thing is silent, you can't hear the birds or the waves.

When do these nights happen? he asks.

You have to be patient, she says. Why don't you go back to bed, you don't have to talk now, let's wait until you get better.

And she presses the switch again, the glass moves back to the sky, she pulls the drapes while Amir, as he has been told, goes back to bed and lies down, closes his eyes and watches the colours caught in a dance, twisted and rippling, of white and blue, green and brown, from the glass to his eyes, from the eyes to the glass.

The woman and the child

Y OU DON'T have to talk, let's wait until you get better. You don't have to leave this room, stay here, just let me know if you need anything. Twice or thrice every day, this is what Rima says and she says this in passing, in an offhand way, but Amir takes it seriously, as some kind of a term she has set for him. Not that this disturbs him, no, because not only does he not know what to say, he likes being left alone. Even if that means lying in bed, looking at the green fibres of the carpet, one by one, for the hundredth time in a day. Or just walking up and down the room, stopping at the window, returning to his bed, falling asleep again.

Now that Rima has shown him how to adjust the glass pane, he can see the city and the sky, in all their colours and their shapes. He tilts the glass at different angles to see sights he has seen before but each time it seems he's seeing them for the very first time.

Like the rivets on the bridge and how each catches the sunlight at a different angle, casts a shadow, a tiny triangle on the massive girders that prop up the city over the river.

The clock tower at the railway station, the smudges on its dial, a bird's nest between the hours three and four, the cobwebs that drag along with the minute hand.

Trucks and cars on the highway that links the city to small towns and then goes on to meet the rest of the world. Sometimes he can see passengers in these vehicles, children in the rear seat looking out of the window.

He likes to scan the Maidan, make sense of the dots Rima told him about, some moving, some at rest.

The sea and the gulls, the crabs and the waves, he's yet to see. That only happens on some special nights, Rima said. He will wait.

As for Rima, she comes in with his meals three times a day, sits sometimes on the floor, sometimes in the chair, watches him eat, clears his plates, adjusts his bedsheet, the pillows, sometimes walks to the window to look out with him and then goes away. Amir can sense that she leaves the house as well, he has heard the main door open and close, the sound of the lift moving up and down. Where and why she doesn't say, he doesn't ask.

But some nights he can't resist switching off the lights in his room, walking right up to the edge, looking at the rectangle of light that spills from underneath her door. He hears her move around, sing, hum a song he cannot make out; at other times, there are voices, someone is there in the room with her, laughing, a man's voice, sometimes a woman, once even a child's, not conversations, merely words, disjointed. Floating on the surface of the deep pool of silence in which the entire house seems to be submerged morning and evening, day and night.

Not that Amir doesn't have anything to say, he has questions for Rima, quite a few. Where is she from? How did she show up at the site of the accident? Why did she bring him here? Does she have a family, a child? Where does she work? Questions, all reasonable, valid, legitimate. But Amir knows he can live without their answers.

The only question he needs the answer to, in some sort of way, direct or indirect, is one about himself: *How long will he have to stay here?* But the few occasions he prepares himself to ask, just when the words form themselves and reach the tip of his tongue, she stops him short: *You don't have to talk,* she says, *let's wait until you get better.* These eleven words, repeated every day, stack up like eleven bricks, one on top of the other, creating a wall in the room, right in the middle, through which he can see her but from where she can't hear a word of what he says. So rather than appear stupid, open and close his lips to speak words that cannot cross over this wall, Amir prefers silence.

And then one night, he has a dream.

He's back in his two-room house in one corner of the dying city, in the building that, from the street outside, looks like a crying face. It's early morning, May or June, and the sun waits, set and determined. As if in revenge for being banished the entire night. He's walked into the kitchen with the two buckets of water he's filled at the Corporation tap on the street below. It's going to be a long, hot day, he can't afford to run out of water. So before he goes for the next refill, he needs to store all of it, he needs to pour the water out of the buckets and into the containers in the kitchen, fill all the glasses and the jars.

That's when it happens.

At first, he doesn't notice, he's been doing this for so long that it's now become purely mechanical. Also, what's there to notice, you are only pouring water into containers, the only thing you have to be careful of is that you don't fill any pitcher right up to the brim since you could end up spilling some water.

He takes a jug, fills it from the bucket, begins to empty it into the jars, one by one, with nothing on his mind except stray thoughts. Like how many people were in the line at the tap today, which shirt he will wear to work. But when he has filled more than half a dozen jars, he hears it, the sound of bubbles.

At the bottom of each full jar, there are two people, a woman and a girl, curled up, pressed flat against the insides, he can see them move inside the water, call out his name, tiny bubbles leaving their mouths, rising to the surface.

He stops and looks into the bucket and sees nothing except water, a few specks of dust floating. He picks up one jar, the woman and the child inside. Holding it far away from him, he pours the water out, back into the bucket. The jar is empty; the woman and the child are gone.

He does the same with the next jar until he's left with only one that has the two people at the bottom, the woman in a sari, the child in a red dress. They claw their way up through the water but so narrow is the jar that they get intertwined, their tiny fingers scrape the glass, leaving thin scratches in their wake. The girl is crying, he can make out her tears in the water, on her face near her eyes, she is the first to drown, he can see her lying, her dress drenched, sticking to her body, like a drop of red paint stuck at the bottom.

The mother dives to pull the girl up but on her way down, she gets stuck too, the ends of her sari float, swirl around her face, strangle her neck.

Amir picks up the jar and pours the water into the bucket but this time, the two don't disappear, they lie there at the bottom, lifeless and wet.

Amir shivers, it's early in the morning, minutes after sunrise but the kitchen has gone dark as if it's evening, a cold wind has begun to blow from somewhere, someone switches the lights on. He turns to look, it's Rima, she's standing at the kitchen door, smiling. Why are you emptying the glasses and the jars after filling them up, she asks, don't we need the water?

He wakes up with a start. His heart races, the glass in the window is tilted up so all he can see through the drapes is the blackness of the night sky. He must have moved in his sleep, he can see the blanket on the floor, the pillow in one corner. His head hurts, he tastes the taste of broken sleep.

No, I'm not in my kitchen, he tells himself, I'm here in Paradise Park, there are no buckets here, no water to pour, no water to store but the dream has filled him with a vague sense of dread. He sits up in his bed and without any effort a plan shapes itself, in neat, logical, simple steps, a plan that appears to him to be the most practical course of action.

He will leave Paradise Park.

I will leave Paradise Park, he tells himself.

I will leave Paradise Park, he repeats.

But not now, only when he gets well, when he doesn't need the pills or the doctors. He tells himself that he has no reason to feel guilty or obliged to Rima, perhaps it was she who was responsible for the accident in the first place. So he'll make the best of the circumstances. He will leave only when he's ready to leave.

The sole issue that needs to be addressed is his absence from the post office. Because he has never taken a single working day off, Mr Sarkar must be worried. Amir is worried about his customers as well – in another week or so, he's not quite sure, he will check the date with Rima, the month will end, they will come back again with their money and their letters for him to write. What he needs to do, therefore, is to let Mr Sarkar know, without telling him where he is because that would complicate things, that he's ill, that he will be back soon.

He needs to talk to Rima to find out a way in which he can send a message to Mr Sarkar.

Thus prepared, he waits for the morning, avoiding sleep so that he doesn't have to see the woman and the child again.

The wounded crow

LOOK WHAT I found in the Maidan, Rima says, walking into Amir's room in the morning with a bird in a cage. When she puts it on the table, beside the bed, Amir can see it is a crow. Someone sawed its beak off, she says.

The crow lies flopped on the floor of the cage, on a shred of newspaper that Rima has spread out, its edges curling around the bars. Its beak is two short black bits, each jagged, cut bluntly at the end, one slightly longer than the other, a white dribble at its base mixed with what must be the bird's blood. Congealed and clotted.

I saw it on the grass, she says, trying to pick up a tiny piece of bread which it couldn't grasp with its beak. The bread kept slipping, it used one foot to hold it and then tried but even that didn't help, it kept pushing it farther and farther away.

The person who did this, she says, must have held the bird's head with one hand, chopped its beak with the other. Why do you think he did this?

Amir keeps looking at the bird, doesn't know what to say because he is still watching last night's dream play in his head. His resolve to confront Rima sits at the tip of his tongue, the words ready to tumble out but he fights hard to keep them back. The woman and the child lie at the bottom of the glass jar, both dead. He can see Rima standing at the kitchen door, smiling in the dark, mocking his fear. He closes his eyes, opens them again, turns to look at the window.

Rima doesn't notice all this, she's busy with the bird.

Can you see how weak it is? she says, not looking at Amir.

She puts the cage on the carpet and opens its door. There is a click, a rustle as the crow flutters for a second. Its legs scrape the newspaper, and then it lies still again, its eyes covered by a thin film reminding him of a sparrow that had once entered his room, flown straight into the moving blades of the ceiling fan, fallen on his bed, bleeding.

Rima's now sitting on the carpet beside the cage, her legs folded underneath her so that the underside of both her feet are what Amir can see, the ends of her blue dress, crumpled, half-covering her ankles. She keeps looking at the bird, her toes twitch, involuntarily. Amir can see her heels, the light criss-cross lines in the skin which fade away to a smoothness, plain, no lines at all. Like a little girl's feet.

Like the feet of Mr Sarkar's daughter, when she sits on his floor, on the cracked concrete, one leg folded, the other propping her up, her fingers around the coloured pencil. It was a teacup, he remembers, she had problems drawing the handle, she couldn't get its curve right. He wasn't good at drawing either but he had tried to help. He told her to picture the handle as a question mark sticking out of the surface of the cup. Draw the question mark without the dot at the end, start from the cup, go to your right and then come back to the cup again, the question mark has to end there, don't lift your pencil, do it in one stroke. Then draw a double line along the same route, that's to show the thickness of the handle, then fill the space between with whatever colour you want. She had tried but it didn't work, the question mark started right but ended a short distance from the cup, broken. She used her eraser to rub it away, brushed the flecks away, the crumbs falling near her feet, the same smooth feet. Like Rima's, a bit smaller.

Don't stand there just like that, Rima breaks his thought, your legs will hurt, you are still very weak, come sit beside me.

It hurts as he bends down to sit, his legs in front, his feet in blue socks, the doctor said you need those, especially in the mornings, the pills lower the temperature of the extremities, he didn't know that word, good that the assistant explained it later, it means hands and legs, we don't want you to shiver, we don't want any reaction.

He sits down, he's behind her now, he looks at the nape of her neck, the hair, smooth and black, falling in one wave. He can see the curve of her back holding the dress, the white stretch between her neck and her shoulder like a handkerchief draped over the clothesline of her collarbone.

She has the bird cradled in her hands now, out of the cage, one of its wings is spread out, its beak against her breasts. So close is the bird that he can smell it, the iron of the cage, the droppings that have dried, crusted on the newspaper. Her hands envelop the bird like petals, white against black, its down between her fingers, like the carpet between his toes.

Here, why don't you hold it for a while? I'll go get some water and milk, it must be starving.

Amir isn't prepared, he fumbles as she passes the crow from her hands to his, their fingers brush against each other.

The bird doesn't seem to notice this change of place, it settles down in Amir's hands, he can feel the beak, its jagged ends, against his chest through his shirt. Rima leans forward, closes the wing that is still spread out and walks out of the room.

Amir shifts to adjust himself so that he's sitting more comfortably on the carpet, so that he can hold the bird without any fear of dropping it. The crow looks frail, I should feel protective, he thinks. He looks down at the bird but feels nothing, just an emptiness filled by the meaningless sensations of smell and touch, the feathers scraping against his hands as he moves them, hard; the little head, soft, rubbing against his thumb and his fingers, the cage by his side, empty, its door open.

If you are afraid of heights, ladies and gentlemen, I have nothing to show you, the man's voice, he can hear the words in his head, loud and clear. But sitting in Paradise Park now with a crow in his hands, the coincidence isn't what strikes Amir, what bothers him is something missing from this recollection, something else about that afternoon that he should remember but he can't. He tries to think harder but it keeps eluding him, reminding him of the day he dropped and broke his thermometer, and as he tried to pick up the ball of mercury from the floor it had kept slipping from his fingers.

OK, let's feed him now, Rima says, entering the room with a bowl of milk in one hand, water in the other, a dropper floating in the glass.

She sits down, asks him to hold the crow while she parts its beak and drops three drops of milk into it. She closes the parted beak, the bird moves and then settles down again. The fourth drop falls on Amir's hands and Rima wipes it away.

Suddenly, it falls into place.

That fragment of memory which had broken and fallen off, that piece which he was trying so hard to grasp: the mother and the daughter in the crowd around the man with the crow, they were exactly like the ones he saw lying dead at the bottom of the water in the jar of his dream.

His hands jerk.

Steady, says Rima, I'm almost done, let me feed it a couple more drops, then we can put it back into the cage.

He sees the mother lift the child to get a better view of the bird and that entire afternoon begins to unfold before him, frame by frame until he can see, right here as he sits in Paradise Park, holding a wounded crow in his hands, the scene in every minute detail: the girl in her shirt, smudged and dirty, looking at a shop window, pointing out to her mother a doll in a red dress, the crowd clapping as the man jokes about the crow, throwing the half-rupee coin, the child entering the shop and the shopkeeper, without saying a word, asking her to leave, even what he later conjured up when he returned to the post office, the mother telling the girl to study hard, promising to buy her the doll in the red dress.

What are you thinking, Rima asks, putting the dropper back into the bowl which is empty now. The crow rests, its eyes half closed as Rima picks it up from Amir's hands and puts it back into the cage.

Let the cage remain here, on the floor, she says, it won't bother you, will it?

No, that's fine, says Amir and then before he can even think of what he wants to say, he hears himself speaking: I want to ask you something.

About last night, she says, about the dream you had, about the woman and the child at the bottom of the glass jar?

She's looking at him, straight into his eyes, he doesn't know what he should feel. Fear, guilt or both? The bird is lying in the cage, quiet, the light from outside filters through the drapes. And Rima speaks her words as if she had plucked them right from the tip of Amir's tongue.

You talked in your sleep last night, she says.

He avoids her gaze, looks down at the carpet. There's a tiny stain of water that must have dropped while she was feeding the bird.

I was in the next room and at first I thought it wasn't anything serious but then you screamed. I was afraid you might fall off the bed, hurt yourself again so I came here and sat in the chair.

He rubs the water stain with his fingers.

I listened to everything that you said, I heard about

your dream, about the part I have in it, that I was standing at your kitchen door, smiling. Don't get me wrong, I wasn't mocking you, I was smiling because I was happy to be in your house, to see where you lived, before I brought you to mine.

You told me other things as well, your words were incoherent but, once I got used to them, I could understand. And yet there were times when it broke, mid-word mid-sentence, leaving blanks which I am sure you will fill as we go along. You told me about your house, the power cuts, your walks down Park Street, the auction shop, the post office where you write letters for those who can neither read nor write.

You are like me, Amir, she says, we both like to help people do things they can't do on their own. Maybe that's why we met.

The bird begins to move in the cage, ever so slowly but now that it's been fed its movements are more assured. And in another strange coincidence that neither Amir nor Rima notices, the bird's wings scrape against the bars when Rima pauses between her sentences, as if the crow were listening to her as well, to the woman who had saved it, and was reciprocating her kindness in the only trapped way it could.

You also asked me when can you go home, Rima continues, I'm not holding you back, you are free to go any time you want to but why not stay here until you get better.

You are still weak, I could make that out last night. Your wounds are healing fine but just give it a few more days. And if this makes you feel any better, I have sent a letter to Mr Sarkar this morning, you gave me the address last night, Shimla Post Office, saying I am your friend and you are ill and that you will be back in a week.

Amir listens, each word pushing him one step forward towards an imaginary precipice between guilt and shame so that he now stands at its edge, can see the chasm beneath, dark and inviting.

Why don't you go back to bed? Rest for a while, you don't have to talk, let's wait until you get better.

That sentence again, but this time it doesn't bother him at all, in fact it sounds as if he's hearing it for the first time.

So he goes back to his bed, lies down, and she pulls the covers over him. He likes the feel of the bedspread stretch under his body as she sits down beside him. She puts her hand on the dressing on his forehead; you are warm, she says, maybe you should sleep now.

Her hand moves down the rough cotton bandage, draws a line along its edge, moves to his chin and his lips, up the face again, and when she reaches his eyes, her fingers brush against his eyelids.

I am counting your eyelashes, she says, do you know how many you have?

He shakes his head in a no, she whispers the count one by one, leaving long pauses in between, during which he can hear the bird in the cage on the carpet and by the time she reaches eight, nine, ten, he begins to slip into sleep, a woman sitting by his side, a wounded bird on the floor.

He has a family, of sorts, he thinks.

Days, nights later

Playing in Paradise Park

THIS IS THE GAME of colours, says Rima to Amir, in which we both undress and lie next to each other, we shall keep all the lights switched on because we need to look at different parts of our bodies making neat little pairs: my knee your calf, my chin your neck, my finger your ear, my toes your shin, so on and so forth. And then you have to describe what you see, I won't look, I shall keep my eyes closed, listen to you and try to guess what you're describing, which part of our bodies you are referring to. Do you understand?

Amir doesn't quite understand.

But he says yes. For he wants to know more about Rima.

What exactly he wants to know he's not sure of but of one fact he's certain: ever since that morning when Rima told him she had listened to him talk in his sleep, that she had entered his dream as well, he knows that while his book has opened itself without him knowing, letting her read page after page, even what lies between the lines, hers has remained closed, its pages all sealed, bound, tucked away in some shelf he can never find.

He has tried asking her questions but she has evaded them all in a manner so natural and disarming that instead of making him angry, it fills him with guilt that in some way his questions don't deserve an answer.

So when she says, do you understand? he says, yes. And decides to play along.

Rima is white.

White as in white, like a towel in a hotel, a bedsheet in a hospital, the pillowcase at home. She's a woman of this city, born and raised here, she says, no link whatsoever with any foreign land. He's asked her twice about her complexion and both times she said no, you must be joking, I have no foreign blood in me, maybe I'm just short of blood. Or maybe I lack the pigments I should have.

As for Amir, he's brown, no adjectives needed. You are brown like wood left in the sun, drenched in the rain, she says. That's why we need to play this game.

Let me give you an example and she locks her fingers in his. Look, bring your eyes closer, look at our fingers, what do they seem like?

Two sets of fingers, says Amir.

No, it's wool, white and brown, each thread magnified, perhaps fifty times, to the thickness of our fingers. Knit into a sweater by some old woman, perhaps your mother or mine, wearing glasses, sitting in a chair on the balcony on a winter afternoon, two balls of wool beside her, one white, one brown, linked by their threads to her knitting needles No 8 No 9 going *click click click click,* a tube of cold cream on the table, its end curled up, twisted.

Amir wants to tell her no, he doesn't remember his mother ever doing that but he checks himself, he has already told her a lot more than he should have.

Then Rima asks him to climb onto her, drape himself over her entire frame. They are almost the same height so she uses pillows to raise herself and tells him to put his head between her breasts, stretch his arms over hers, lie still. That way, she says, if you're on the ceiling looking down, it will appear you are a dark brown shirt, with long sleeves, spread out to dry against a white sky, the clothesline running below my collarbones, my nipples the two pegs holding the shirt at the shoulders.

The only white on Amir's body, besides the acid streaks on his fingers, are the three stretch marks on his left shoulder. They have been there for twenty-five years, he has used them in dozens of application forms when he had to mention his distinguishing physical feature.

But no, Rima says, turning to Amir, you are wrong, those stretch marks weren't there when I first met you, when I saw the doctors clean your wounds. I have too much white in my body, she says, and because we sleep together, snuggling against each other, your shoulder pressing against my back, a bit of my extra white, the white I don't need, drips out, night after night, streaking your shoulder drop by drop. Like tallow melting from a candle.

Amir can tell her stop lying, stop making these things up, but why, he closes his eyes, turns to her side and tells her yes, she's absolutely right, his white is hers, the stretch marks were never there until she picked him up from the accident and brought him to Paradise Park. Changed his clothes, washed his blood away.

Now it's your turn, she says.

Close your eyes, he says, picks up a pitcher of water lying on the bedside table, closes the fingers of her right hand into a fist and then half-dips it in water.

A woman is standing at the bottom of a canal, he says, she's searching for something, it has rained and a lot of water has collected there, there's no way she can cross without getting her feet wet. This woman looks around and, as luck would have it, she sees five bricks arranged like stepping stones so she hops from one to the other. The stones are pale white in colour, her feet are brown, when she reaches the last one, she jumps to the other side, dry and warm. What am I talking about, he asks.

Your finger counting my knuckles in the water, she says.

Her eyelashes blinking in his cupped hand are the wings of a dragonfly as it tries to escape from a glass bottle.

Her nipple in his ear is the plug that shuts out all the sounds except that of the blood in her heart.

Her breath on his face is the wind in the summer.

And so they play.

Describing and naming, naming and describing different parts of their bodies until one of them falls asleep, the other follows, sometimes they make love, the lights still switched on, sending Amir back in the room on Free School Street, his eyes fixed on the newspaper in the prostitute's window where the pane should have been, her clothes in a big coloured heap on the floor, the marks on her legs, the welts on her back and the night of the accident when Rima brought him to Paradise Park.

The second game is a kind of show and tell, both sit in front of the window, tilting the glass by turns, looking at the city in new ways.

Amir shows her the crowds, their clothes stained with sweat, people whom Rima has never seen. For example, a family of three in a house beyond the Maidan, the father staring out of the tiny window, his glasses lying on the newspaper crumpled in his lap, his back towards his daughter who's writing something, the mother in one corner, sitting on the floor, cutting vegetables.

Rima shows him the sky changing colours, from white to blue to red as the sun sets on the Maidan, the clouds, stray and scattered, white and grey, like the drops of milk she fed the crow that morning.

As night falls, Amir tilts the glass to face Park Street, tries to show her a man weaving his way through the crowd stopping once in a while at shop windows to look. A woman holding a child, wrapped in the end of her sari, running to the cars that pull up in front of the restaurants, the child fast asleep, the woman holding its hand, tapping the glass with its fingers.

They wait for the night to fall and then she turns the glass around, away from the city, away from everything he has seen and shows him the sea. At first, it appears not much different from the sky, black with huge patches of purple, but she adjusts the glass, brings a mop and wipes it clean, tilts it a little this way and that. And there it is:

the water, the white specks of foam, the gulls flying in low circles around the waves, the moon glinting. Or is that a street lamp along the beach, its neon light making the sand seem like white powder?

They make up little stories as they go along, Amir and Rima, and then they fall asleep on the carpet, the wounded crow fast asleep in its cage, the glass fixed at the sky, the drapes pulled away so that moonlight floods the room, makes the green carpet seem like white sand near the sea.

Some nights, Rima says we shall tell each other what we want and we have to make it happen, any which way.

One day, he tells her how much he wants to go to a place called Shimla, he tells her about his favourite pictures. Of the snow he has seen in the shop window, the pine trees lining the narrow road which turns and twists in the hills. She listens carefully, brings out cotton wool, dips some of it in cold water, spreads it across the living room floor, on the green carpet. That's the snow, she says, as she turns the air conditioner to maximum so that a chill floods the room. She lights a fire in one corner, brings out winter clothes, shawls and jackets, gets a small iron bench, like they have in parks, and they both sit on it, her head resting against his shoulder, his fingers in her hair.

Another day, Rima says let's go to a foreign country, to a café where we can sit and talk, like lovers. And she colours her hair blonde and both of them set up, in one corner of the room, what she calls an American diner, complete with neon lights, a red table top, ketchup and mustard in red and yellow plastic bottles with nozzles, paper napkins in steel holders, salt and pepper in shakers.

She puts a doll on the far side, she's the waitress, says Rima, as she turns into a character from a book she says she has just finished reading. Or a movie she says she has seen.

One night, Rima is someone called Kathy and she says that because she's been treating Amir's accident wounds, she will make Kathy a nurse at a hospital who works long hours.

She asks Amir to play David, the man who's in love with Kathy and they meet after she gets off her ten-hour shift at the hospital, past midnight, the only other customers are two dolls, big and small, Rima says that's the mother and her baby.

She gives him his script, which she has written, complete with instructions in brackets as to what he needs to do when he reads the lines.

I know my lines by heart, she says.

And they act out scenes:

Kathy and David sitting at the table, David holding her hands, touching her nails, the pink half-moons at the bottom of each, the red nailpolish.

David asking Kathy to marry her.

Kathy saying she needs some time to think.

Years later, David and Kathy, man and wife, are back in the café, both are looking at the baby fast asleep two tables to their left, the mother staring at her coffee, the baby by her side, half on the couch, half on the lap.

When they reach home, their little daughter lies fast asleep, the covers are off, Kathy and David both pull the covers over the child and switch off the lights. Then they walk out into the parking lot, he kisses her on the forehead and holds her close.

Over her shoulder, her hair brushing his ears, Amir can see, through the glass window, the dull glint of the railway line, there's no train at this time, his eyes move inwards over the sad roofs of sad houses, from this height, the tears, the dampness, show up in little patches of seepage. Rima washes her hair, puts all the props back, the three dolls that served as the waitress, the mother and the child. Amir helps her clear the table and, looking through the glass now, all he can see is the darkness crawling across the Maidan towards the window.

Rima makes a request

AMIR IS HAPPY, his wounds have healed, the bandage is off, the doctors have stopped coming, the pills are over, there's not even the faintest mark to show that one night there was an accident. Once in a while he remembers the post office, Mr Sarkar, his house, his walk down Park Street, the disapproving glances from the men who run the auction shop, the guard at the housing complex telling him to move on, not stand there and stare at the children perched on the iron gate using it as a swing. But these are now more like pictures from a past he's put away in some corner of his memory. Knowing very well, in fact this is what Rima keeps telling him, that he can, at any time of his choosing, leave Paradise Park and retrieve them.

It's this awareness of the lack of permanence about everything around him that not only gives Amir a courage he has never known before but also helps him look at Rima in a whole new light.

He had started off convinced that lying there on the tramline, wounded and hurt, he had filled her with overwhelming pity and that there was no way he could repay her kindness except perhaps through gestures of gratitude, awkward and absurd. Like lying in bed with her, playing along, making up words for different parts of their bodies.

Looking out of the window at the sky at day the stars at night; trying to slip into the skin of strange characters he would never meet. In strange places he would never go.

However, watching Rima closely in Paradise Park has made Amir aware of her true nature: that she has holes in her heart she needs to fill every day, be it with someone like him, a stranger hurt in an accident, or a crow with its beak sawn off, holes he can never even plumb the depths of.

That's why he lets so many of his questions remain unanswered. He decides to scrape only the surface, contented in the little details that Rima lets slip: her face lit by the green light when she bends down and opens the fridge, the soft sounds she makes in her sleep, how the bread crumbs dandruff the front of her nightdress in the morning, drops of water and milk sliding down her fingers as she feeds the crow, the way she tucks her hair behind her ears.

And that's why one day, when Rima makes a request, let's go to your house, I want to see where you lived, I want to live there for a few days, he doesn't suspect anything, doesn't think twice, says yes, let's go, not the least bit aware that moving out of Paradise Park, even for a short while, could be the beginning of the end.

It starts with a walk along the driveway.

The beginning of the end

No, there was no wall, he's sure of that. Amir and Rima are walking in the driveway of Paradise Park, around which a wall is being built, its construction apparently started after Amir reached here because, however hard he tries, he cannot recall the wall from the first night, he can see only himself hurt, the blood streaming down his face, the shards of glass caught in his skin, looking through half-closed eyes at Rima's ankles, the ends of her sari, the driveway black in the night, spotless and gleaming, but no wall, there was no wall, he's sure of that.

Rima says they decided to build the wall to keep the crowds away because they collect on the street outside, every day, around this time on their way home from work, naked and well dressed, hungry and well fed, all waiting to look at this building.

Most of the wall is ready with a few chinks here and there, each a couple of feet in length, just a few inches across, sections yet to be walled up or those that have cracked before the stone and the cement could set.

Wait for just a second, Rima says, I think I hear something, it's a child crying. Let me look.

She bends down, sits on her haunches, presses her face flat against the chink, squints for a better look.

I can see the street outside, she says, a bus passing, I can see some feet, I can hear the child but I cannot see anyone.

Amir stands behind her, he can see her back, her hair, her small shoulders as if she were a girl who has dropped something on her way home from school, is picking it up.

Why don't you look, too? she says. It's so different from what you see through the window.

She moves aside, still sitting, clearing a space for Amir who sits beside her, the driveway is clean, he doesn't have to bother about his trousers.

So used has he become to look from the heights above that his first view in days, from up close and down below, is a blur. Of large shapes and sizes. He blinks once, twice, to adjust his eyes and then he can see the patch of the pavement outside, crumpled pieces of paper, black water in the drain, a pair of feet walking by in torn slippers, a woman's feet since he can see some nails coloured. Exhaust from a passing truck makes his eyes smart, he coughs.

OK, Rima says, enough for one day, let's go. Did you hear the child crying, she asks.

No, he says, because all he can hear is the sound of her shoes, their soles slapping the hard, unbroken tar, darkened by the wall's shadow that paints a sweeping arc of black across the driveway.

Amir looks at the wall.

Four feet thick, it rises more than thirty feet in the sky in a steep incline, curving upwards before it travels all around the driveway. It's made of brick, painted dark grey, like an overcast sky, care has been taken to ensure that the lines of the bricks don't show so that to all outward appearances, it seems that the entire wall has been carved out of a single, colossal piece of granite.

On top of the wall, all along its perimeter, are shards of glass, brightly coloured and sharply cut, alternating with black iron spikes: a fence perhaps meant to strike both fear and admiration in the hearts that race and the eyes that watch.

Caught in the glass and the spikes at several places are pieces of clothing, tattered; in some places, there are strings as well, with stones tied at their ends, flapping away in a breeze that has begun to blow from across the Maidan.

Some people never give up, Rima says, they must have tried to scale the wall but couldn't get over the spikes.

What happens to these people, Amir asks.

I don't know, she says. Maybe they are arrested, then released a few hours later with a warning or two. Maybe they jump down, their clothes torn, their skin scratched, go back to where they came from.

They keep walking past sand, cement and stone chips, piled in three hillocks in one corner, creating a wet-dry valley in which sit a group of construction workers, men and women, their hands caked with sand. A woman walks by balancing an iron tray on her head, loaded with cement, Amir can see her tired eyes through the end of her yellow sari that covers her forehead.

That night, the dream of the woman and the child comes back again, several times. Like pieces of glass seen through a kaleidoscope, the dream arranges, rearranges itself, yet looks very much the same, a part of the same disturbing pattern.

First, he's pouring the water, the woman and the child are in the jar trying to break free, calling out his name in bubbles, rising to the surface, clawing the water, making it swirl in tiny eddies and ripples. Then, there's no jar and no water, the woman and the child are in his room, lying in his bed, he can smell the dampness on their clothes, feel them move, rustle in his sheets.

At other times, he sees them in a crowd on the street, the child looking at a shop window, the mother dragging her away. Sometimes they appear, through the tilted glass window, as two tiny dots on the Maidan, looking up at him, waving, forcing him to recoil in fear, sometimes even hide.

And in all these dreams, Rima is always there, either standing at the kitchen door, smiling, or beside him on the bed. Or walking along a street, on the other side, entirely unaffected. As if to her, nothing of this dream matters, neither the past nor the future because her journey begins and ends in the present.

Wake up, she says, let's go, I'm ready.

Rima is standing at the door. She has one bag slung across her shoulder, another in her hand. She's also holding the iron cage with the crow, its beak seems to be healing.

Where, Amir asks.

To your house, she says, resting the bag and the cage on the carpet, walking to his bed. You wanted me to see your house, didn't you? I want to see where you lived,

I want to live there for a few days, maybe a week, and then we will come back.

When do we go, he asks.

Tonight, she says, we shall take the last tram from the Maidan, that way we will escape the crowds. No one will notice me in your neighbourhood.

Yes, says Amir, let's go, only dimly aware that bending down to look through the chink in the wall, the sound of the child crying, the sound he could not hear, his dream, and now Rima's decision to leave Paradise Park, take him home, are all in some way connected.

A faint foreshadow of things to come.

Back home

THEY GET OFF across the street in front of Amir's house and when the tram pulls away, empty, except for the two sleeping conductors, dragging with it the pool of light that spills out of its windows on either side, Amir and Rima are left standing in the dark. There's a power cut in the neighbourhood. It's complete, on both sides, even the street lights are off, though here and there shadows flicker through the windows, some closed, some half-open, from candles and lamps.

It should come back soon, Amir says, the power, they can't have so much darkness for so long a time.

It may rain tonight, Rima says.

He looks up to see clouds, dark and low, almost touching the topmost branches of the banyan tree across the street. There's a light breeze that brings little comfort since it blows the heat across Amir's face, wraps its hot fingers around his neck, drips a line of sweat, warm and wet, down his back. But it stops short of Rima, leaving her face dry, fresh, not a single drop of sweat. As if over her dress she's wearing an invisible layer of air, cool and heavy, that doesn't allow the heat to enter.

Hold my arm, Amir says, as they climb up the stairs in the dark, two full flights. She is holding the cage with the wounded bird, he her bag. When he unlocks the door to his house, Rima lets his arm go, standing behind him.

When he steps inside, his feet touch the buckets, both of them, still exactly where he had placed them before he had boarded the bus for Park Street on the evening of the accident. As usual, he had closed all the windows when he left but the air inside is fresh, he smells the heat but no musty scent. His fingers brush against the small palm tree he keeps in an earthen pot, the leaves feel fresh as well. Has someone watered them in his absence? Or did it rain so hard that water entered through the balcony, curved around the wall, reached the plant, drenched its leaves? He can see the flecks on the floor, those Mr Sarkar's daughter left behind when she rubbed the line in her drawing away, he runs his fingers against the armrests of the chair, they leave no lines in the dust. It's as if someone moved into his house in his absence and lived here, exactly like him, moving out only moments ago when he and Rima began to climb the stairs. Or as if he left the house, not for days and nights, but just a couple of hours.

Or maybe it's nothing, Amir thinks, as he tells Rima why don't you sit here, pointing to the bed, you must be tired.

Rima waits behind him, she doesn't move.

How could he have forgotten, this is the first time she's here, she doesn't know where the bed is. So he holds Rima's hand and guides her forward, but to his surprise, she needs no guidance, she walks as if the room were brightly lit. Without him telling her, she avoids the plant in the corner, puts the cage between the two chairs and sits down on the bed.

Give me a second, he says, and walks to the kitchen to get the lamp he has so carefully polished, prepared for nights like these.

I can't find the matchbox, he says.

Don't worry, I have one, she says.

They sit on the bed, his lamp ready to be lit, its glass glinting in the dark, the oil up to the brim, a fresh wick trimmed. Rima says why don't we sit like this, in the dark and wait for the power to come back? But Amir wants to light the lamp – he doesn't want the darkness to conceal from Rima the imperfections of his world into which she has just stepped. Because he wants her to see it all, to see the speckled cement on his floor, cracked like skin in winter, he wants her to see the stains in his toilet, the bottle of acid by the side, he wants to prepare her before the morning light floods his house. So he takes the matchbox from her, lights the lamp, opens the window, so light is the breeze that the flame of the lamp hardly moves. And in its light, he shows Rima the patterns he can make with the shadow of his fingers on the wall. A dog with its tail sheared off, a crow flying, its beak cut. He asks her to join him at the window, lifts the drapes and points out the black street and the black night. Look, he says, there's my sea, pointing to a puddle of water that has spilled from an overflowing drain onto the street. And like she does in Paradise Park, he moves his window, its small pane, points out to her how the reflection of the lamp's flame changes shapes in the smudged glass.

Rima laughs.

He puts a finger on her lips, says quiet, we don't want to wake anyone up.

They lie in bed, she rests her head on his chest, it's a narrow bed, one side pushed against the wall. This way, he says, it's safer for two people, less chance of one of us falling off during sleep.

Listen to the night, he says, you don't hear these noises in Paradise Park. Forget that rustle for a while, that's the bird in the cage, you have heard it before.

Footsteps: someone walking on the street outside.

A creak: Bomba, the boy upstairs, must be turning in his bed. He tells her about him, about how he plays cricket every afternoon, dragging the maid along against her wishes, how he has asked him to get foreign stamps from the post office.

Scrape: perhaps the cockroach in the drain. Or the bird in its cage.

Snap: a bit of the lamp's wick, the burnt part curling.

Rima is silent, Amir runs his fingers over her eyes, can make out that they are closed.

Click: the fan has begun to move, the power is back.

It's still dark when he wakes up, her head is still on his chest, there's a pool of sweat under his neck. He cradles her head with his hands so that she doesn't feel him move away from beneath her, adjusts the pillow's height and then guides her head onto it. She moves, he holds his breath, she doesn't wake up, he's standing beside the bed now as she, still asleep, puts her left hand across her eyes perhaps to shut out the light from the street lamp outside that's marked a thin line across her cheek, down her chin, down her neck.

He walks to the window on tiptoe, closes it, shutting the light out but her hand doesn't move. Curled up, her fingers hold the matchstick, burnt, with which he lit the lamp. He lets it be, maybe she will drop it during her sleep. Far away from Paradise Park, in his own house, she looks more vulnerable and Amir feels, in a way he cannot understand, a momentary reversal of roles. As if she's the one wounded. And he, eager to heal.

He enters the kitchen. Maybe a week, Rima had said, but there isn't even stuff for a day. The red plastic basket in which he keeps the vegetables near the gas cylinder is empty except for a few potatoes and onions, their skin shedding onto the floor. The frying pan sits on the gas stove with the lid on, there are potato fries there, he had cooked that last evening. They should have gone bad, the oil, the potatoes, but he can smell no stale smell. Anyway, he will throw it out in the morning, he decides.

On the shelves there is oil, salt, pepper, spices, every-thing that he needs so all that he has to get is the rice, the flour and the vegetables, maybe some eggs. He will make breakfast for her.

But first he needs to get water, he needs to be there before the others in the neighbourhood come because he doesn't want anyone to ask him where he has been all these days, he hasn't thought of an answer yet, he hasn't made up a lie he can safely repeat without missing a beat. So he picks up both the buckets, opens the door, again slowly lest she wake up, and walks down the stairs to the Corporation tap.

He's too early, the tap is still dry.

He puts the buckets on the street and waits, looking around. It must have rained during the night, but only a drizzle, since there are no patches of water on the street, just a light wetness that covers everything. Nothing has changed in his absence, the shops, their fronts are still the same, he can see the same dog, brown, its tail little more than a stump, curled up in the space between two wooden cots on the pavement on which two men lie asleep. He looks up and into the distance in the direction of Paradise Park, but there's nothing there. Except the tram wires hanging low, the sky, at dawn, stretched out, like a huge cloth to dry, over the iron, asbestos sheets of houses.

From across the street, he can see a wisp of smoke where the tea-stall owner must have woken up and started preparing for the day, boiling a big kettle of water. A taxi passes, rattles, noisily coughs its exhaust. He's afraid Rima may wake up, wishes the taxi could gather speed, disappear.

The tap stutters water. It will take a while, ten or fifteen minutes, before it lets flow a steady stream. As the first bucket half-fills, he can see the children of the sweetshop owner, the brother and sister, both with two small buckets each. They line them up, the girl counts the buckets aloud, one to six, four of hers, two of Amir's, the boy rubs sleep from his eyes.

*

When Amir reaches home Rima is up, she has watered the plant, opened all the windows even the one he always keeps closed – the one in the kitchen – because he's afraid the draft will extinguish the stove flame. But now that she has opened it he can see what he has never seen before: a corner of the building, dark, through which the water pipes go, plants growing from beneath, two sparrows playing in circles around their nest behind the pipes.

You have seven stains in your toilet bowl, Rima says.

She laughs as he begins to pour the water into the jars in the kitchen, the sun is up but it's still not hot yet, its soft white light flooding the kitchen. He remembers the dream of the woman and the child trapped, swimming in the water, but as he fills the jars one by one he sees nothing unusual.

When he's finished, he turns, Rima's standing at the door, smiling, just as in the dream.

See, everything is all right now, she says, you are back home.

Amir wants to show Rima around his neighbourhood, the post office, the cinema hall, the bus stop, the man with the crow, he wants her to stand in the crowd with him, listen to him talk about Paradise Park. But the man isn't there today, instead at the same place, there's a crowd watching something else: a man swallowing a fish.

The man is on his knees holding a fish which wriggles in his fingers as he pops it into his mouth. He gulps, walks all around, his mouth wide open, to show everyone that the fish is gone, that it isn't sticking to the roof of his mouth or hiding deep inside, behind his teeth.

The crowd applauds.

The man turns towards a little girl, her hair matted, her face streaked with dust and tears, she is his helper, he says. Get me the water, he says, I can feel the fish jumping inside, if we don't give it water, it will die and then the show is over.

She brings him two buckets full of water, one by one, hands him a glass. Turning to the crowd, he says count the number of glasses I drink, please count them out loud.

And he drinks and he drinks and he drinks.

One, two, three, four, five, six, Amir looks at Rima who isn't looking at the man but at the little girl who stands by his side.

The man stops at seventeen to a round of applause.

Stand away, now, the man says, the fish wants to get out. I can feel him inside, he's a happy fish now, he wants to meet all of you so I have to let him come out, he is so happy he is dancing in the water, up and down, up and down.

An uneasy silence grips the crowd as it moves backwards, unsure of what may happen next.

Let's go, Rima says, I don't want to watch this.

Don't worry, says Amir, it's nothing, it's just a trick.

The crowd moves back as the man, holding his head high, as if all the water were in his mouth, walks towards the edge of the pavement.

I am now a tap, he says, thrusting his head forward, lowering it at a right angle to his chest so that it's parallel to the ground, his mouth right above the drain.

He stands perfectly still and lets the water flow. The crowd watches, someone claps, the squeamish ones turn their heads, Rima is looking at the girl who's now playing with the ribbon in her hair, looking at the dirt in her nails, oblivious to what's going on.

The human tap runs for a full two minutes, all seventeen glasses, and then the man stands up, coughs once, closes his mouth with his hands, walks around the crowd and then brings out the fish, still alive, writhing, drops it into the bucket.

He talks to the fish, sorry, my friend, he says, I kept you in the dark for so long, now you are out in the light, among your friends. The girl picks up the bucket and takes it around showing the fish alive and well, swimming in the plastic bucket.

Let's go, Rima says.

They pass the Bombay Dyeing store where he shows her the line of air conditioners. So thick is the crowd now that Rima and Amir can't walk side by side as waves of people pass by taking him a few steps ahead one time, her at another.

Their next stop is a man selling a pictograph, a set of brightly coloured drawing instruments, transparent circles and triangles made of plastic with several holes drilled in lines, parallel and elliptical. By arranging them, moving different coloured pens in different holes, he draws lines on paper, spirals and circles, blue, red and black that first seem like scribbles and then begin to form patterns, complex, geometric, beautiful.

They pass the pavement stalls selling blouses and scarves. An old man calls out to Rima, Didi, we have a blouse for you that will match your sari, make you look even more beautiful, Rima smiles, moves on.

They walk past the cinema hall, through the evening crowd, past two men in black selling tickets, mumbling two for twenty, two for twenty, stop once in a while to look at other things: a man selling parrots; rabbits in a cage, their eyes glinting in the dark like green sapphires; tiny boats that move on the water in a small tub if you light a little candle inside.

On their way back home they stop at the post office. It's late in the evening so it's closed but Amir wipes the dust off the big glass window, cups his hands to shut out the light from the street and shows Rima the chair he sits on, the desk where he writes. The candles are still there, so is the bottle of glue, the sticks of wax, just like he had placed them that afternoon.

The sound of a child crying

THE ELECTRICITY is there when they return home but they don't switch on the lights as they undress in the dark, in the cool breeze of the fan, smell the city on each other, its heat and its dust, the man throwing up the water, the fish writhing in his hands, the coloured spirals forming themselves on paper.

Give me a second, Rima says, I need to wash and she walks into the bathroom. Amir hears her pour water from the bucket he had filled in the morning, listens to the splashes on the red cement floor. He hears the sound of the mug as it slips from her hands, falls, she picks it up, the gurgle as the water rushes in to fill the mug when she dips it into the bucket, a splash again. She dries her hair standing in the middle of the room, spraying drops of water on Amir.

Later, lying in bed, they listen to the sound of each other's breathing, the rustle and scrape of the crow which seems to have healed since it has begun to fly inside. Then they talk like two children planning the first few days of their vacation, hurried and breathless, one after the other, one not even waiting for the other to finish the sentence.

I will come to the post office tomorrow as a customer, Rima says, I will walk to your desk and you will write a letter for me. I will speak out loud, people will be surprised why I'm getting you to write the letter when I can write my own, just imagine their faces.

During lunch break, we will go together, Amir says, to the man with the crow, and when he has finished his act, we will step out of the crowd, walk up to him and say that you live in Paradise Park and that no crow can reach that high. That he's lying, making things up.

Then they make plans for Park Street and he says he will show her the stalls which sell foreign goods, the auction shop, the mirrors as big as the wall, objects from hundreds of years ago, from the homes of kings and queens. He tells her about the shop attendant who gets angry if you don't buy anything and she says don't worry, we shall give him a surprise, I will buy new props for new games to play when we return to Paradise Park.

He tells her about the children playing with the iron gate, the cement divider outside the hotel where they have planted flowers and trees, the posters in the trams with all those stories about trams in foreign cities – Paris, Berlin, Vienna and Moscow. They will board the tram from where it starts so that she can get a seat right up front, not the Ladies' Seat at the back, so that she can read the stories.

Yes, she says, yes to everything that he says.

And it would seem to anyone that they are settling down to live happily ever after but a strange little thing happens in the night: Rima wakes up hearing a child cry.

At first, she thinks it's in her head because didn't she

hear it while walking along the driveway in Paradise Park, through the chink when she bent down to look, but this time it's louder, clearer, as if it's coming from the room next door.

Amir has told her there's nothing in that room except a spare bed so it must be from the street outside. She gets up, the pillow slips to the floor, its thud too soft for Amir to wake up, she draws the curtains aside to see where the crying is coming from, looks this way and that, right and left, but sees nothing.

Except, of course, the black night and the black street. And a dog.

What happens next, we know.

Rima is gone

WHEN AMIR wakes up, Rima is gone, never to return, leaving nothing behind. She's even taken the bird in the cage. He searches every corner of the house: he looks at the bedsheet to find some wrinkle, any crease left on the pillow; he scans the floor countless times, maybe there's some mark somewhere, perhaps from the birdcage, perhaps she dropped something on the floor, the burnt matchstick the night they came from Paradise Park.

He goes to the bathroom, searches for her smell, the marks of her fingers on the soap, some wet piece of clothing she left behind. Seven days and seven nights is a long time she spent here, she cooked several meals but everything in the kitchen looks untouched, there's nothing to show she was here.

Amir returns to work at the Shimla Post Office where no one seems to have felt his absence. Or, if anyone has, no one mentions it. Mr Sarkar stops by his desk on his way to the bathroom, says, I hope you are feeling better. The customers come, clutching their money and their stories, Amir wraps them both, seals the flaps.

And like every day, every evening, he returns home, teaches Mr Sarkar's daughter, picks up from where they left off – still struggling with the handle in the drawing of the teacup.

He takes the bus to Park Street, walks past the shops which sell smuggled goods, the auction shop, watches the children play on the iron gate using it as a swing, meets the prostitute again on Free School Street above the photo studio, walks across the Maidan to take the tram home. Nothing has changed.

He sees huge piles of sand, stonechips and cement, standing like three hills in the night, and in the valley formed by them, he can see construction workers resting after their long shift.

Excuse me, which way is Paradise Park, he asks, they lower their heads in respect and maybe fear, they look at him from head to toe and then they get back to work, mixing the cement with the water, emptying the stone chips into the roller which spews black smoke in the night sky.

Amir looks around, across and beyond the wall to see the Maidan's expanse, the tank and the barbed wire fence, there are no children playing at this hour.

He waits for the tram to appear around the corner, to stain the darkness with its pool of light, and hopes that he will get a window seat so that waiting for the accident, one more time, he can rest his head against the frame and look in the same direction as he and Rima did not long ago. Through the tilted glass of Paradise Park.

The tram whines to a stop, its bell clangs, he gets up and walks to the window seat. The tram starts with a shudder, he lurches forward, has to hold the edge of his seat to balance himself, and as he settles down, feels the engine vibrate under his feet, he can hear a child crying, the sound coming from outside the tram, in front.

As the tram moves, slicing the darkness of the Maidan with sharp yellow knives from the headlights, the sound begins to get louder and louder, until he has to press both his hands to his ears to muffle it, to shut it out somehow. But he can't.

So he lets it be, rests his head against the bars of the window and allows the crying to lead him forward, carry him home.

END OF PART ONE

THE SECOND PROLOGUE

'I thought I heard her crying,' says Father. 'Has she eaten?'

Father's sitting at the dining table, he asks the question without raising his head; Mother, standing two feet away, answers without raising hers.

'You don't worry,' she says, 'she and I will have dinner together.'

'Is she all right?' Father pulls the chair towards the table. Its wrought-iron legs scrape the cement floor, making a noise that Mother doesn't like.

'No, it's nothing,' she says. 'Don't worry, she got drenched in the rain today, she must have caught a cold.'

I can now hear what they say since I'm circling lower down in the sky, so low I can even hear the child crying. And what I earlier saw as tears in her eyes have now marked lines on her face. I can hear her drawing her breath, short and sharp. I can hear little hiccups from her little chest.

'Get me some salt,' Father tells Mother.

She walks back to the kitchen.

The salt is kept behind the spice jars on the wooden shelf that runs along one side of the wall. Mother has to get onto a chair to reach it. She cleaned the shelf this morning, removed the old newspaper stained with oil that

dripped from bottles, marked with the fine dust of spices
that have fallen from jars – turmeric, cinnamon and cloves.
Making lines coloured yellow, green and brown.

I'm near the kitchen window now, the crow doesn't
make a noise although it's flapping its wings very hard to
maintain balance, to stay aloft in the air.

Through the glass of the window, fogged by grime and
dust, I look over her shoulder.

'Do I have to wait for the salt until dinner is over?'

Mother hears Father shout from the other room, hurriedly gets down from the chair and walks back with the
salt.

The crow and I pull back. We have to remain unseen,
unheard.

'Where is she?' Father asks.

'She must be on the balcony,' says Mother.

He sprinkles the salt onto the rice, the vegetables,
sprinkles so hard the grains fall outside the plate. Marking
the dark brown wood of the table with flecks of white.

Mother stands a few feet away, leans against the wall,
watches him eat, watches his lips, his tongue move over
his teeth, roll the half-chewed food. It's been more than
ten minutes since he rinsed his hands in the bathroom
before he came for dinner but the water hasn't evaporated.
She can see the hair on his wrist still wet, the strands all
parallel, pressed to the skin, across a light-coloured band
marked by the strap of his watch, the one he bought the
day they were married. It's a Hindustan Machine Tools
watch, it shows the day of the week and the date, its

second hand has a tiny plane at its tip, moving round and round.

The wind blows stronger, the curtains on the balcony flare up like a maternity gown with no one inside. It will rain harder tonight. Mother can feel the cool draft on her face.

Let Father finish his dinner, she thinks, then she will walk to the balcony and ask her in. She can hear the wind gather strength, rattle the window in the kitchen, rustle the ends of the newspaper as it claps against the shelf. She hopes the wind doesn't topple the jars over. She can feel a coolness at the base of her head, beneath her long and thick hair as if someone has lifted it for a moment and is blowing gently on the nape of her neck.

Father's done, he gets up, pushes the chair back, walks to the bathroom to wash his hands, she can see the marks his fingers have left on the plate.

She wipes the table with a mop, picking up the scattered salt and the rice grains that fell from his mouth as he talked, carries the wet mop back to the kitchen, along with Father's plate.

Chandra, the maid, will come tomorrow and do the dishes.

On the way, she shivers. Maybe it's the sudden rain-laden wind that's entered the house. Or maybe she's afraid.

PART TWO

you are afraid

Once upon a time in the town

ONCE UPON A TIME by the side of the highway that links the city to the rest of the world, a couple of hours as the crow flies, there was a small town, and in this town, they said, they found the body of a girl, eleven or twelve years of age, lying at the bottom of a canal, twenty-five feet deep and as many feet wide.

To reach this canal you have to take a narrow road that veers off the highway, as if by accident, like a dead branch in a tree. This isn't a road exactly, it's not even a dirt-track beaten hard into shape by feet after feet; it's more like a passageway created on its own. Half mud, half slush, meandering between two straggly rows of houses, marked in several places by pools of black water, which run from either side, water that's been thrown out of houses after washing and bathing. Water mixed with the soap and grime of dishes and men.

In the city, they call something like this the service lane, the neighbourhood's most neglected stretch, choked with garbage furtively packed in plastic bags or newspaper wraps, tossed from windows on either side which are opened for only this purpose and remain closed for the rest of the time. No one wants to see the service lane, even acknowledge its presence, although they all know that it performs the most important task of them all: it keeps the houses from rubbing against each other.

And, sometimes, late at night, it offers space for trucks to sneak in and out when they come into the neighbourhood, violating the city's laws, to dump construction material, sand, stonechips and bags of cement.

But in this small town, it's different. This clearing between the houses serves as the road, and if you are new to the town, chances are you will find it difficult to walk down its middle. Your slippers will sink, the slush will splash, mark your trousers, especially if they are black.

The best thing to do, therefore, is to go there in the winter, if you need to go there at all, when there is no water in the sky or the air, or even on the ground; when taps are dry, when people, wrapped in sweaters and shawls, have as little to do with water as possible. Even then, people here will suggest you don't take this road and, if you have to, walk along its margins, where the ground is more stable and hard.

If you keep walking for fifteen, twenty minutes until the houses end, you will reach the edge of a canal which runs at right angles to the road, before it takes a sharp turn to encircle the town. Lining one side of the canal is an embankment of earth in which plants grow on their own and beyond this is the highway which, as we said earlier, leads in one direction to the city and in the other heads for the rest of the world.

Why and how the canal came to be here, no one knows. Some say that long, long ago this was imagined as a stream running around the town, brimming with clean, fresh water with trees on either side where people would come and rest in the evening, sometimes paddle in brightly coloured boats. But nothing of that sort happened, now this is little more than a ditch, very long and wide, littered with dead leaves, overgrown grass, sprawling patches of water hyacinth, shards of metal, twisted and bent, bicycle rims, rusted chairs which have served their purpose, the daily refuse of houses.

Until the rains come, children come here, without their parents, to slide down the canal's sides and play, hiding and seeking among the piles of garbage, rummaging to see if they can retrieve something, anything, to sell as scrap. During the monsoon, however, water collects, heavy and foetid, its stink enters the houses to sit on clothes, sometimes on bedsheets and wet towels. And since the air is humid, the water takes a long time to dry, the stench stays for days and days until the town gets used to it. Like a patient in a hospital bed who soon learns, without any effort, how to live with the smell of disinfectant, the doctor's gloves, the starch in the pillowcase, even her own sick breath, things she wouldn't have tolerated when she was healthy.

And so it is on one such morning in the month of July when the sky is ashen, slapped hard by thunder, sick with crying the monsoon rain, when the stench of wet earth hangs all around, that a woman called Mala, a newspaper reporter, shows up in this town from the city.

To find out who the girl is. And how and why she was found dead in the canal.

*

When Mala arrives there aren't many people at the bus stop, just two men who don't even turn to look at her as she gets off. There's a bag slung over her right shoulder, she raises the bag over her head to keep herself from getting wet and runs the couple of steps to a tea stall where she finds a place to stand, in front of a bench. It's a wooden plank resting on two legs made of six bricks each, one stacked on top of the other.

The bus leaves. She can smell its black exhaust and see a thin rainbow film of oil it has left behind, snaking on the wet road. She looks at her watch, two raindrops have spattered the dial, so she wipes them away. It's a few minutes past nine, the entire day stretches before her. Like the highway from the city she's just travelled on.

She sits on the bench, waits for the rain to tire itself out to a drizzle.

In front of her, against the mud wall, sits the man who owns the stall, he's behind an oven, his face half-hidden by the huge aluminium kettle, its sides as black as coal, licked by flames, blue and yellow. Behind him, on a small earthen shelf carved into the wall, there are three plastic jars, all identical, one packed with biscuits, the other with assorted chocolates and lozenges, their shiny wrappers dulled through the jar's dirty plastic. The third is half-full with sugar which is obviously for the tea since the owner keeps bringing it down, putting it back again.

Mala can hear, from above, the rain drum the tin roof of the stall, the water and the milk boil, the hiss of the gas and the clink of glasses and spoons as a little boy washes them, his shirt drenched with sweat and rain. She watches the owner use a brown towel as a filter, wring the tea out, open the towel to empty the leaves back into the kettle. The little boy takes each washed glass, shakes it dry and places it on a tray, lining up the glasses in rows of four each. Then he takes the tray to the owner who checks whether the glasses are clean, if there's any drop of tea still clinging to the bottom. Once he nods his approval, the boy puts the tray on the floor by the side and stands near the gas oven looking at the kettle, waiting for his next instruction. Mala can see the rain fall on the back of his shirt, his hair.

She should have brought an umbrella, in fact the sky was overcast when she had stepped out of her house but it was only when she was in the bus more than ten miles away from home that she remembered she had forgotten it. Through the window, she had watched the clouds travel and wished that by the time she reached the town they would have gone far ahead. To other towns and cities down the highway. But perhaps the bus had been fast, it had caught up with the clouds so that it dropped her off just when they had begun to empty themselves out.

She asks for a cup of tea although she doesn't want one, but sitting on the bench, she has begun to feel a bit guilty. From her bag she takes out the sheet of paper that someone in the City Hospital gave her.

It's your map, he said, the report of the girl who was found dead in the canal, that's all we have.

The boy comes with the tea, puts it on the bench in front of her. The steam rises from the glass, warms her face as she unfolds the sheet of paper and begins to read. One more time.

The post-mortem report

THE POST-MORTEM REPORT is a single sheet of photo-copied paper, handwritten on both sides, the edges dark where the original must have folded over while being scanned in the Xerox machine, the black ink running in the margins, maybe there was something wrong with the toner in the copier, the shopkeepers always cut corners, never replacing it until the customers start shouting. Mala isn't the kind to shout or complain. There's a signature and a seal at the bottom, both of which are so smudged that she can't make out anything except the number seven in the date meaning the month of July.

This is the month of July so Mala feels reassured, the report couldn't be made up.

She got it after bribing the hospital attendant fifty rupees who then said, I'll give you this sheet of paper only for half an hour, read it, take notes, you could get it photocopied, I need to have it back before anyone notices. He guided her to a nearby studio on Free School Street called 'Flash Express' where, besides taking pictures and selling film, they also had a copier. Above the studio, her friend in the hospital said, are prostitute quarters, this is the red-light district, so please be careful.

She didn't have to worry, the job took less than five minutes.

She sips the tea, it's too sweet, she makes a face which no one notices and begins to read the report once again. The rain has let up; another five minutes, she guesses, and she should be moving. She looks at her watch, the dial's dry but streaked where she wiped the water drops away. She reads:

Subject: Post-Mortem examination and expert opinion about the dead body of female, eleven years old, vide FIR No 232 dated 16.7.01. Under Section 364/302 of the Indian Penal Code.

Body found in: Canal, one and a half kilometres north-east of the highway, at the end of the road in the town.

Body brought and identified by: (name illegible).

Deceased last seen: On the night of 14 July and police got information about dead body on 16 July at 6.15 p.m.

Examination of body: On 18 July at 11 a.m.

Length of body: Four feet four inches.

Clothes and ornaments: Red-coloured frock, short sleeve; white underwear, metallic earrings.

General condition of body: Foul smell present, maggots of size 1–1.5 cm crawling over body.
   Bloating of features, peeling of epidermis, hair easily comes off, nails fallen, teeth slightly loose, blood-stained frothing from mouth and nostrils, eyes protruding.

Right hand: Middle, ring and little fingers have gnawed effect.

Injuries: There is bruising of the lips and tongue.

There are multiple abrasions of various sizes and shapes on upper limbs and back of body.

Scalp, skull and vertebrae normal.

Brain and spinal cord liquefied.

Thoracic walls, ribs, cartilage normal.

Pleural, larynx normal.

Lungs have blackish marks.

Heart softened and flabby.

There is a bruising of the pharynx. A gag is present as folded handkerchief which is checked in colour. Gag is completely blocking the pharynx.

Stomach contains food material (small quantity) including pieces of onion.

Small intestines contain digested food material and gases.

Large intestines contain faecal material and gases.

Liver, spleen, kidneys softened.

Bladder contains about 100 ml of urine.

Organs of generation: There is bruising of the labia and bruising of the vaginal walls and tears of the anterior vaginal walls.

Opinion: Cause of death is gagging, time since death is about three and a half days and there are signs of struggle and sexual intercourse.

Handed over to police: Dead body, copy of report, police papers duly signed, clothes in a packet, all three sealed and stamped, vaginal swabs with three samples for semen detection, ornaments with two seals and three samples of seals.

The boy has taken the glass away, Mala looks at the tiny ring it has left behind on the bench, brown and broken. She looks at the streaks in the wood, it must have been left out in the sun and rain for a long time, someone has carved a name on it, she likes things neat so she wipes the ring away with her palm, wipes it dry against her bag.

She has packed light, she plans to stay here for only a night.

Is there a hotel here, she asks the tea-stall owner who has poured another feed of milk and water into his kettle.

In the market, he says, near the hospital. They have two or three rooms, clean but very small. Why do you want to stay there?

I'm from a newspaper, she says, I have come to find out about the girl they found in the canal.

He's wringing the filter again.

Do you know anything about it? she asks.

No, Didi, he says, I haven't heard of anything.

Which way is the hospital? she asks.

Walk down this road, it's at the end of the market. Be careful, there's a lot of slush, walk on the side, the ground there is harder, you have chosen a bad time to come here.

To the hospital via the market

THE WALK TO the hospital is via the market, and at this time of the morning, because of the rain, although it's now only a drizzle, there aren't many people out except vegetable-sellers. They are lined up on both sides of the road, makeshift stalls on the narrow pavement, standing beneath umbrellas, their wicker baskets draped with sheets of plastic, dirty white or dark grey. Like the wet sky and the wet road. The only flashes of colour Mala can see are when the edges of the sheets flap in the gusts of wind and rain, fold over, revealing for a moment purple brinjals, orange pumpkins cut into two, their yellow fibres wet, watermelons, their black seeds dotting the red and the pink, green tomatoes, most of them small. This isn't the season for tomatoes.

The only ones who seem unmindful of the rain, who have nothing over their heads, neither umbrellas nor plastic sheets, are the men who sell fish. As if by letting themselves get wet they can wash their guilt over bringing the fish out of the water. And so in one last gesture of generosity, they let the rain fall on the fish as well: the catfish, the mackerels that slap around in large, shallow aluminium tubs, whipping up a thin soapy layer of froth. The bigger ones, the hilsa and the rohu, are kept out of

the tubs, dead, in glistening rows on wooden tables. Mala
can see their eyes. Her mother told her once that if the
eyes glisten, the fish is fresh; if they are glazed with a film,
they may not be fresh. So point that out and get him to
bring the price down.

Fresh fish, a man calls out to Mala.

He is old, she can see above his vest his veins wrapped
around his neck like ropes to keep his ancient ribs from
falling apart. He's wearing glasses. This strikes Mala as
odd since it's unusual for a fishmonger to wear glasses.
His lenses are wet in the rain and tied with a string coiled
around his ear instead of the frame.

Didi, the man next to him calls out, please stop for a
minute, I'll show you what we have, just for you, fish
straight from the river, caught this morning.

Mala walks on, looking straight ahead. She remembers . . .

It's evening.

She is walking in a market, a covered market with a
roof, white tube lights fixed in the rafters. She has walked
past the vegetable section and is now in an aisle that
separates two red raised cement platforms on either side
where fishmongers sit, in two long rows, each with a huge
block of ice by his side and a large cutting knife held
between the toes. She's careful, trying to avoid the slippery scales on the ground, the wet entrails, tossed away
for the dogs and cats that live in the market's shadows.
The overhead lights are switched on but most stalls have
their own lamps, which hang down from the rafters, their

yellow light draped over the dead fish. That's their strategy, her mother had cautioned, look at the eyes carefully before you fix the price, these men keep a light bulb on top so that the eyes gleam even if the fish have been dead for hours. And the ice is there to hide the stale smell.

She's halfway down the aisle when the lights dim, a chill tugs at her hair, brushes its fingers across her face. She turns to find out what's happened: the stalls are exactly as they were, the lights are still on, the fishmongers are still shouting, calling out to customers, she can see their lips move, their faces break into smiles, she can see the customers stop, look at the fish, part the gills, push and prod, bargain or walk away to another stall. But everything is silent.

The only sound she can hear is that of her breath, of her lips as they part in fear because instead of the fish, she can now see that they are selling corpses, of men, women and children, all naked and dead. Except for a few babies, the size of mackerels, which thrash around in aluminium tubs, the soapy film sticking to their tiny heads, plastering their thin, wet hair. Instead of the scales and the gills on the floor, she can see clumps of hair and nails, some polished red. She walks faster, she slips, a man she cannot remember reaches out to hold her steady. The lights dim further, the chill is now almost a freeze . . .

Didi, look where you are going, a man says.

Mala has bumped into him. He's with a girl, perhaps his daughter, who's holding the shopping bag and looking at the fish.

She snaps out of it, says sorry. The man walks past, the child looks at her once and then turns away.

Mala walks on, why did she remember that? Forget it, she tells herself.

The leather bag over her shoulder has kept her back dry. The bag is zipped tight, the leather is coated with some kind of waterproof material, she doesn't need to worry. She has brought one change of clothes; she will stay for only one night.

Behind the vegetable stalls, she can see the shops, shuttered, their corrugated doors pulled down, fastened by locks that touch the pavement, wet in the rain. They will all open in an hour. She reads their signs: 'Singla Medical Store', 'Classic Art Gallery', 'Nancy Readymade', 'Sharda Beauty Store', 'Prem Sweets'. All have their addresses painted as well – Hospital Road. She feels reassured, she's on the right road.

The drizzle has stopped but the sun takes its time to appear. The rain is reduced to threads blown by the wind; fine, like the spider's web on the wall at home. People have begun to spill over onto the streets from the shelters in which they waited. Children on their way to school, in groups of three or four, girls with ash-coloured skirts and white shirts, boys in trousers and shirts, the same colour combination with dark grey ties that come with ready-made knots. Some of them have raincoats with plastic hoods pulled over their heads, the straps of which they hold at their necks since there are no buttons. The wind is strong, making the raincoats flare over the bulge of their schoolbags.

*

Mala doesn't have to ask anyone for directions to the hospital since she can see it up ahead. Right by the side of the road, two huge iron gates and an enormous poster on the wall. The poster is yellow, the writing in big black letters, each the size of a baby, reads: *Small Family, Happy Family.*

The hospital is a sprawling structure, a single storey that looks deceptively imposing from the outside with huge white pillars and red-tiled roofs. She walks through the gates up what seems to be some sort of a driveway, past groups of patients and their families waiting for their turn, past a fruit stall conveniently located right near the entrance so that visitors can buy bananas and apples for their relatives inside.

She walks up the flight of stairs to a landing where there's a sign pointing right, to the room of the RMO, the Resident Medical Officer. On the wall is a wooden board streaked with rain that must have dripped from some crack in the ceiling. It has the names of all previous RMOs and their dates of service, beginning with the year 1969. That's the year she was born.

The current one is Dr B. K. Choudhury, MBBS (Cal.), MD (Cal.), 1999 to present. Her family doctor was also someone called Dr Choudhury who died last year, a distinguished-looking man, always in a white starched shirt and black trousers, his silver-grey hair brushed back, highlighting his glasses, which had thick, black shell frames and made him look, even at the end of a long day, in summer or in winter, as if he'd just stepped out of the shower, clean and fresh. His hands always smelled of Dettol, his face shaved close, scrubbed, not a single sweat stain anywhere, his room and desk spotless, uncluttered, no dust, no loose paper, even his prescription written in so neat a handwriting that she could make out all the names.

Dr Choudhury, her mother told her, was the one who was there when Mala was born and eleven years later when her father died.

The doctor isn't in, says the orderly, a man between thirty and sixty years old sitting outside the RMO's room, unmoving, as if invisible ropes tied him down to the plastic chair and its iron legs.

Where's the patient? he asks.

No, I haven't come for any patient, says Mala, I have an appointment with Dr Choudhury. That's a little lie but it doesn't matter. I just need fifteen minutes, she says.

What's it about? he asks.

The girl they found in the canal.

Which girl? What about her?

I have the report, I want to ask him about it, maybe she was Dr Choudhury's patient.

That she could very well have been, most of the people in this town are. But what can he tell you? You should meet the Post-Mortem Man, he must be the one who opened her up, he opens all the bodies here.

Two women appear in the corridor, they walk to the orderly and ask for the doctor.

He snaps at them, have I kept him hidden in my pocket? Can't you see he's not in? Just wait outside, I'll tell you when he's here.

Where is this Post-Mortem Man, Mala asks, what's his name?

His name you don't need to know, we all call him Post-Mortem Man, he's been doing this even before I came here. Go and talk to him. Provided, of course, he's sober because that man is always drunk, morning day and night, though you can't blame him given what he does every day.

Let me first meet Dr Choudhury, Mala says, I don't know when next I can meet him because I have to return to the city tomorrow.

OK, do as you wish, Didi, why don't you go and wait inside?

He holds the curtains aside to let her step in and, without moving an inch in the chair, points her to the doctor's table, to another chair. She sits down and he lets the curtains fall. She's alone in the room.

A table fan blows a cool draft across her face. She can feel the sweat and the rain on her back, her jeans wet against her ankles, her shirt sticking to her back.

Across Dr Choudhury's desk, there's a World Health Organization calendar on the wall with the picture of a baby being given polio drops, its face wrinkled into a cry, its head resting in the crook of its mother's arm, her bangles beneath its back, the doctor's gloved hand over its mouth.

To the left of the calendar is a chart, handmade, showing the number of children in the town who have been given polio drops and the total number of children. All letters and numbers are in felt pen, blue and red. Blue for target achieved, red for what's left to do.

Mala looks at her watch, it's ten past ten now, the

time they show in all watch advertisements. She adjusts the chair so that she faces the fan straight on, the uninterrupted draft begins to dry the water in her hair. She puts her bag on the floor, she will change when she reaches the hotel. Once in a while, the curtains billow in the fan's wind and through them she can catch glimpses of the orderly still sitting in his chair, his head drooped low, his hands in his lap, staring down at the floor, maybe he's asleep. A man with a child parts the curtains, peeps inside, sees no one in the doctor's chair, disappears. She can hear the sound of the child crying.

Mala can feel her eyes close. She woke up at four in the morning today, the walk from the tea stall to the hospital was a long one, it must have been at least a couple of kilometres, and her shoulders hurt from the bag's strap. Now the fan's drying her sweat, covering her with a coolness that begins to lull her to sleep. She tries to keep her eyes open by staring at the pen-stand on the desk, two ball point pens, one pencil, the paperweight, its glass chipped in three places, sitting on a prescription pad. There's a bit of a candle, lying on its side, must be for evenings when there's a power cut. She gets up to stretch her legs and walks across the room to a tiny window in the corner, which opens out into a yard that, evidently, hasn't been used for ages. She looks through the rusted, iron bars but there's not much to see except a tiny patch of green, wet in the rain, dead leaves, used syringes, a plant with two leaves and some cotton wool stained red. She returns to her chair, it's nearing eleven, over five hours since she left home and she has got nothing yet, not even a sentence, to add to what she already knows.

She can feel the first wave of panic begin from somewhere in her stomach, like a knot tied tight and then slowly unravelling on its own. She closes her eyes and waits, this time letting sleep wash over her like water, cool and clear.

Didi, let's go. The orderly is standing beside her, Mala wakes up with a start.

It's lunchtime now, the doctor sent a message saying he won't be here until later this afternoon, he's out on call. But I have brought the Post-Mortem Man here, he's free, why don't you go with him. Ask him your questions and then on the way back, stop over and see Dr Choudhury. Give him a tip, whatever you think is right, not much, that's all he needs.

It's past noon, she has slept for an hour, she can feel the dull ache in her neck – her head must have leaned over to one side and stayed that way for over an hour – and her lips are dry.

She gets up, picks up her bag and follows him out of the door, they walk down the corridor, turn left at the landing and there at the bottom of the flight of stairs, stands the Post-Mortem Man, the first person in the town who's going to tell her something about the girl in the canal.

As if on cue some clouds have cleared. The sun beats down hard but can't dry the air, still wet, laden with rain.

The Post-Mortem Man

WHAT DO I TELL YOU, Didi, except for myself, no one here wants to touch the dead, not to mention cutting, cleaning them up, stitching them back, in fact, no one wants to do the simplest of simple things, which even you can do if I show you how. Like raising the body's hands and legs, letting them fall, looking at how they drop down to check if rigor has set in. You don't believe me, Didi, go and ask anyone in the hospital, Dr Choudhury himself, the head nurse, the senior doctors and surgeons who come here on their inspection trips once every two or three months from the district and sometimes the city, go and ask them who is the Post-Mortem Man, is he of any use? They will tell you, and I'm not saying this in praise of myself, they will all tell you, we need him, we can't do without him.

The Post-Mortem Man pauses but only to catch his breath, goes on.

I know where all the internal organs are, I know what's required as viscera samples, where the cerebellum is, the liver and the spleen. I can, without any X-ray, without looking, feel the ribcage and tell you even if one bone is chipped and all this when I haven't been to any school or medical college, I can't read or write. When I have to send letters, I have to pay extra at the post office for a man to write them down. My name, I can just about sign, I learnt that only a year ago, on my own, until then, it was my thumbprint when I got my salary. But if there's one thing I have learnt, Didi, it's this. In my line of work, experience is what counts, not expertise.

Let him go on, Mala tells herself, let him run out of things to say, then ask questions.

Most of the time, doctors don't even step inside the room. Maybe because of the smell, because the bodies usually come hours after they have been found. Or maybe they are afraid that blood, little pieces of flesh, will splash onto their shirts, washed and freshly ironed, especially when I have to open the scalp with the knife, peel it back, crack open the skull with a hammer and a chisel. So they stand outside, looking through the window, I keep telling them what I see, they note it down in their papers, in the certificates they need to sign. And then they tell me stitch it up, stitch it up Post-Mortem Man, make it quick, make it quick, the family's getting impatient, they are waiting to take the body away.

He walks only a little slower than he speaks so Mala almost has to run as she follows him across the hospital lawn, in the centre of which is a lamp post that's toppled over although its cement base is intact, rooted to the ground. The post, about fifteen feet long, meant to stand vertical, is now a long arch, like one of the supports in a bridge across some river or along a railway line. It serves as a rusted iron clothesline for the hospital staff who live in one-room quarters in a corner of the campus; the Post-Mortem Man, being a Dalit, lives separately. In the middle, where the fallen lamp post curves five feet clear of the ground, children have slung an old tyre that they use as a swing. He crouches, walks underneath the post, brushes against the tyre which begins to swing. Mala follows.

She can see his shoulder blades through the shirt that sticks to his back in large dark patches of sweat and rain, his hair cut close. His black trousers are torn near both the knees, the seam of one leg has come unstitched, his shirtsleeves are rolled above his elbows where the skin is furrowed and wrinkled. His heels stick out of his rubber slippers which must be at least two sizes under, his nails and toes are caked with mud.

When Dr Choudhury's orderly first introduced her to him, she had asked about the girl in the canal, to which he had said, Didi you first need to see where I work. Look around and then ask me whatever questions you have. I have met many reporters.

Can you see it, he says, the building where I work?

He has stopped, so suddenly that she almost bumps into him and smells the liquor on his breath. The clouds have begun to gather again, the sun is gone, the wind waits to blow. She looks in the direction in which he's pointing.

The small building, red in colour with an asbestos roof that gleams in the half-light of this half-afternoon, looks abandoned, squatting in an empty plot more than five times its size as if every other building, in front or back, right or left, wants to keep a distance from this one.

Why is there nothing around? she asks.

Whom do you blame, says the Post-Mortem Man, this is where corpses come, at least once every day, on many days twice, between ten in the morning and six in the evening. Who will want to live here?

Maybe that's why, Mala thinks, there are no children playing here although the wall of the house could easily have served as a readymade cricket stump, its vacant plot large enough for an eighteen-yard pitch. Even for a game of football, if you have five, at the most six, players on each side.

Mala looks down just in time to avoid a large puddle and by its side she can see more reasons why no one comes here: there are signs of the dead wherever she looks.

White cloth that's begun to turn yellow, perhaps torn from the winding sheet over someone's body; clumps of hair, a pile of marigold flowers, dried and brown; incense sticks, some half burnt, some unused. These must have dropped, by accident, without anyone's knowing when someone's body, dissected and stitched up, was being taken back to the pyre . . .

Marigold flowers, incense sticks, she is eleven years old, standing on her balcony, too short to be able to see over the edge so she raises herself on her toes, presses her face against the iron railing, looks down at the yard below, where Father lies on a wooden cot, a white sheet draped over him, tented by his feet at one end, stretched tight up to his neck. They have unwrapped and lit a whole packet of incense sticks, she has never seen so many of them at one time except during the Pujas when they did that in front of the idols. The ash falls on Father's head, on the white sheet, on the bright yellow marigold flowers strung in a necklace, ringing his face. Someone has taken two of the smaller flowers, placed one on each of his eyes. Mother is crying, without making a noise. The women of the neighbourhood hold her, her head leaning against one of their shoulders.

There are people Mala can recognize, her uncle, aunt, another uncle who has come by train to be here this afternoon. She wants to cry at her father's death but she can't. Someone lifts her from behind, says poor girl, she didn't deserve this, losing her father at so young an age. She wants to say that she is happy she won't see Father any more but she looks at Mother cry and that makes her cry as well and her tears mix with the dust on the railing, marking her face . . .

Didi, Didi, he says, are you listening? Last year we had a fight in the town and three men were killed and I had to work in the evening which is against the law but that was a special case, the district magistrate himself had come, he brought a generator on a handcart and we used that to switch on a light.

Usually, I am done by seven, I have to inform the doctor on duty and only then can I go home. I like the young doctors, most of them come here with plans to change everything. I have seen doctors, Didi, who right from the first day sit in their rooms, day in, day out, night after night, not sleeping, they don't even take lunch break, and when the supply of white tablets, the antibiotics, runs out, they give me money from their own pockets, tell me to get the medicine from the private pharmacy down the road. I tell them, please go home it's too late, no patients come at this time and if they do, I will send my son to your house with the message, but they sit there. And then one morning, it's all over.

They are gone, left for good, resigned, whatever. Moved to a new job in the city, maybe with a large medicine store that has a tiny room at the back for the doctor. Some doctors, I know, sit there in the evenings and then come here two to three times a week only to sign the attendance register. Post-Mortem Man, they say, keep a watch, if the civil surgeon comes to inspect, tell them I have gone out to buy some medicine and will be back in the evening.

I don't blame them. You see, I don't have anywhere to go, my son is already ten years old and he will have to be trained for this job, I will have to be with him until I die, maybe if I die in an accident, he will do the post-mortem of my body as well. But doctors are educated, they have wives and children, how can they stay here? So without thinking twice, I do what they tell me, and in return they pay me something extra, but I tell them, don't pay me anything, just get me a bottle from the city, good foreign liquor.

He smiles.

And at last, he stops talking.

They have reached the building and he brings out the key from his shirt pocket, unlocks the wooden door, his sudden silence so rare that it makes other noises sharper, louder: the clink of the key, the lock, the grating as the bolt slides across the wood, the creak of the door as it swings open. They step inside and Mala's surprised to see it's very neat, scrubbed, not a speck on the floor, no smell, nothing, just dry streak marks, maybe left behind by a mop and water. There is a heap of clothes pushed to one corner of the room: one of a pair of black socks, a towel and a vest, its straps torn.

These are clothes from last night's body, he says. It was a man who had hanged himself. The family didn't ask for his clothes so I kept them back. I will use them to wipe the blood off my hands and the knife, before I wash them in water.

Why don't you look around, he says, I'll be back soon.

The Post-Mortem Man has left, but Mala can still smell his breath and sweat. She looks around but there isn't much to see here. Her eyes are drawn to a small, rectangular tank half full of water, in which she can see a large knife, its blade thick and wide, resting against a chisel and a hammer.

She had imagined, from the shows she has seen on TV, a gleaming steel tray, with more than a dozen surgical instruments, all glinting in a soft, green light, sky-blue scrubs in sparkling steel hangers draped over steel rods washed with clear, boiling water, rubber gloves in sealed packs, but instead she sees a cement platform built in the centre of the room. This is where the body is kept. Red ants crawl in a line that runs almost straight, except for a little bend in the middle, down the legs of the platform on which light falls through the window, bringing with it shifting patterns of green and black, the shadows of the leaves outside. It's on this platform that he would have kept the girl's body. Mala can see the Post-Mortem Man looking at her through the window. He's standing in the backyard with a broom in his hand, clearing something away, but from where she stands she can't see what.

She takes out the post-mortem report from her bag and reads it once again, this time looking for questions to ask when he comes back, but there's nothing. She goes through each line, one by one, the girl lying here, in her *red frock, short sleeves, white underwear.* He must have used the knife to rip them off the body, how would he have removed the *metallic earrings,* did her earlobes tear? The body had been in water for a long time so he wouldn't have had to use the knife real hard, the skin must have given way easily, *the brain and spinal cord liquefied, peeling of epidermis,* she reads.

She had food inside her, *pieces of onion,* Mala will ask him about this, she will also ask him about what he did with her clothes, did he keep any back, is there something missing in the report?

What was the food you found in the girl's stomach?

I don't remember, tell me what the report says.

Onions, she says, to which he replies yes, must have been onions, these things they write down very accurately, whatever I say. Maybe there were bits and pieces of potatoes as well, that must have been her lunch.

What about the clothes, do you remember a red dress?

What will I do with the red dress, I have a son, he can't wear one, can he? He laughs.

I'll tell you what I would have done. If it was a nice dress, not damaged, just wet and torn in a few places, I would have given it to my wife who would make something out of it. If I had a daughter, that's a different thing altogether, maybe she could have worn it or stitched little dresses out of it for her dolls.

Is there anything that you remember about that girl's post-mortem, anything special?

Well, let's see, you say it was a girl, eleven to twelve years of age, how long ago was this?

Just last week, Mala says.

To be frank with you, Didi, I don't remember much, I could tell you all sorts of things but why mislead you, you have come here from the city and you have a job to do.

Mala can feel once again the knot of panic she first felt, in her stomach, while waiting in Dr Choudhury's room. The Post-Mortem Man has nothing new to add, in fact, she isn't even sure if he's the one who saw the girl's body. Trying to hide her anger and impatience, Mala searches for a question, some question to which he can give an answer that will in some way justify the time she has spent with him, listening to him talk and talk.

Where is the canal? That's where they found the body, she says.

The canal? That's very easy, it is exactly behind us but you have to walk all the way back to the main hospital building, back on the road that comes from the market and then take a left turn. You won't miss it, you will see the water, that was the water which must have made her skin soft. You said you are leaving for the city?

Tomorrow, she says.

Well, Didi, if you need to ask me anything, you could meet me again tomorrow morning. I am free before noon.

The Post-Mortem Man locks the door, the frayed

collar of his shirt flaps against his neck, so strong is the wind now. Mala doesn't want to get caught in the rain.

I will be here in the evening as well, says the Post-Mortem Man, so drop by if you have anything to ask me, anything specific, although I don't know what I can add to what you already know. A better idea is to take a look at the canal where they found her. Maybe you will find something there, he says. It will take you ten minutes at the most, you can make it in time, before the rain starts.

She turns to wave at him, after all he did spend some time with her, he showed her the room, but he's gone, must have returned to the yard to finish sweeping whatever he had started to tidy away.

On the way back to the hospital she can see, from a distance, the crowd of patients getting thinner, the man at the fruit stall has covered the apples and the bananas with a plastic sheet and then pressed it down with weights to keep it from flapping.

When the wind is strong, her mother had told her, the clouds get scattered, it takes a little longer for the rain to fall. She hopes her mother was right because she needs to look at the canal before calling it a day, she needs to find something. Anything.

At the bottom of the canal

BUT THERE'S NOTHING HERE. Mala has walked, slid, walked down the side of the canal. She has reached its bottom where there's an ankle-shallow pool of dirty black water into which someone has dropped five red bricks in a straight line, which Mala uses as stepping stones to reach the spot where she thinks the girl's body was found. But there's nothing here. Just plain earth and clumps of grass, torn shreds of paper bags, yellowed and stained. She sits down for a closer look, there are stones of different shapes and sizes, a shiny piece of wrapping paper pressed flat against the ground, the kind that comes with biscuits in a jar.

When she had a fever as a child, twice or thrice every year, usually after the rains when she got drenched on her way back from school, Dr Choudhury would make a house call. He would place the thermometer in her mouth – she liked the warm, antiseptic smell of his hands, the cold bulb of the thermometer against her tongue – while Mother would stand at the door, worried and watching. Father wasn't allowed to enter, so from the next room he would keep shouting aloud: give her biscuits and water, her stomach won't take anything heavier. Biscuits for two days and then she can get back to rice and vegetables.

Mother would bring a tin jar and put it on the bed by her side. Its lid is closed, she would say, but it's not tight, it's very easy to open. Mother gone back to the kitchen, Mala would spend hours looking at the jar, running her fingers over the serrated surface, its floral patterns, red, yellow and green. Then she would roll the jar up and down the bed, she liked to listen to the tumbling sound the biscuits made.

Have one every half an hour, Mother would say, I will keep checking.

Mala didn't like these plain, glucose biscuits; her favourite was the one with cream in the middle, but she had a fever, she had no choice, so she would open the lid, a milk-sweet smell would rush out from the tin jar, the smell of biscuits and wrapping mixed with that of the thin rust on the lid. She would break a bit of one, watch the crumbs collect in a thin fine brown layer at the bottom and then she would nibble. She hated the taste, so with the biscuit piece still in her mouth, she would take a gulp or two of water. Moistened, the biscuit slurry would become tasteless, and just when Mother was about to enter her room, she would swallow the water, close her eyes, pretend that she was asleep. Usually, this worked.

Using her nails, Mala prises the wrapping paper from the ground, puts it in her pocket, just in case.

She hears a rustle from above, the sound of feet against leaves. There are two children, both boys, one of them rolling a bicycle tyre with a stick. When they reach the edge of the canal, they stop and the tyre wobbles for a moment before falling down. They look at her.

She waves, they don't move. She smiles, they don't smile back.

Did you know the girl? she asks, loudly; her voice carries over and above the sides of the canal.

The boys turn and run away, forgetting the bicycle tyre. She hears their hurried steps recede into the distance. Standing up, her knees make a cracking noise – this is meant to happen to old women, I am only thirty-two – then she turns to walk back up, stretching her arms involuntarily to balance herself on the bricks, one leg on each. She can hear the trucks trundle down the highway, cargo trucks, maybe carrying someone's furniture, refrigerator, even a car. Someone who's moving to or away from the city.

One of the boys is back. Questioning has failed, so she tries endearment.

There's a chocolate in her pocket, one of two she bought at the bus terminal in the city. She offers it to the boy but he shakes his head in refusal.

Did the police come here? she asks.

Yes, he nods.

Did you know the girl they found here? Did you play with her?

No, he nods again.

The second boy has now appeared with a woman, old, bent, the keys at the end of her sari slapping against her back. The old woman calls out to the first boy: come home now, don't stand here, it's very dirty.

And all three turn their backs on Mala and walk away.

*

An hour gone, almost, and Mala still knows nothing beyond what the canal looks like. She has seen the houses on either side of the clearing, the spot where the girl was found, the bricks in the water, the two boys and the old woman, perhaps their grandmother, but the boy told her nothing more than what's there in the sheet of paper she has in her bag. The only clue, if it's a clue at all, is the shred of wrapping paper, maybe there was a biscuit in it, which the murderer tempted the little girl with. Like the story of the stranger offering something to the child to win her over, the big bad wolf, the woodsniffers Mother told her about when she was a child. They were men in long, flowing robes, scarves around their heads, pulled down over their ears and their eyes; men who walked around with pieces of wood dipped in some strange poisonous chemical and they first lured you with your favourite things – cricket balls for boys, dolls for girls – and as soon as you got close, they would thrust the piece of wood under your nose, and before you knew it, you were fast asleep, kidnapped.

She begins to walk back up the side of the canal. It's a steep climb and her feet slip against the loose gravel. Back in that clearing between the houses, the canal is now behind her but even as she walks away, its stench stays with her, like a neighbourhood dog which keeps tailing a stranger, giving up only when she turns the corner, away from its sight. Or when it realizes it's not worth the effort.

She sees the old woman again, the woman who was with the two boys. This time she is standing in the front yard of a house, a broom in her hand.

Mala asks: Ma, I am looking for a house, of the girl who was found in the canal.

The old woman keeps sweeping the yard as if she hasn't heard, but Mala can see there's nothing to sweep, it's as clean as it can be. There's a blue nylon cord strung across with clothes on it. The old woman, already bent, passes right under it so that her back brushes the end of the towels and the shirts hanging there, wet and heavy.

Where is the house where the girl lived? Mala asks again.

This time, the woman straightens, looks at her once, points to a house which she has already passed.

The white house? she asks.

No, no, she says, speaking for the first time. It's the red-brick one, the one with the two windows.

Many thanks, she says, but already the old woman has turned her back to her and is sweeping again. Mala can hear the scraping sound of the broom against the dry mud floor in the yard.

The red bricks have long lost their colour so that the house appears red only in patches. There's a yard there, too, the crumbling tiled roof overhangs the wall like a torn hat pulled over its face. In the doorway there's an old bedsheet, frayed and discoloured, that serves as a curtain.

Mala stands there, there's no sign of anyone inside. She looks around hoping she will see someone who can call out to the people inside since she doesn't know their names.

Anybody inside? Mala asks.

No response except from the bedsheet door which swells in the wind. From a distance, she can hear the old woman still sweeping.

She stands there for five minutes, waiting. A crow caws and Mala looks up. The sky is dark but it's cleared in a few places, the sun still hidden. The crow looks strange, as if something is on its back, something that looks like a tiny person, a toy man or a woman. A crow flying with someone on its back? I am seeing things now, she tells herself, what will I see next, the crow land on the roof of this house with the murderer on its back? She is looking at the bird fly in a straight line towards the city when she hears her, sees her hand lift the bedsheet, tuck it in some notch in the wall she cannot see, a woman at the door, must be the girl's mother.

Her father hasn't returned from work in the city, she says. What do you want to know?

I want to know who killed your daughter, Mala wants to say but she can't ask her that right away, it doesn't sound appropriate. So she decides to ask her first about the red dress they found the girl in. Always begin by asking people pointless questions, her mother had told her long ago, a lesson she said she had learnt from Father who worked as a reporter. Because it's only when they think you are stupid that they let slip a secret or two.

The mother and the red dress

So Mala begins: Tell me something about the red dress they found your daughter in.

The red dress? What can I tell you about the red dress, Didi, except that it was her favourite, she wore it only on very special days. We bought it with the money my son sent from the city, his first salary. He works very hard, at a factory where they make shirts only for people who live in foreign countries. He wrote to me saying Ma don't wait, get her the dress, if you fall short of money, I will send you more.

She kept the red dress in the only leather suitcase that we have, where I keep the gold bangles I got during my wedding. From somewhere, she got a page of a newspaper and she tore it in two halves, down the fold, put one on top and the other below the dress, saying these would protect it, keep the dust out.

At least twice every week, at night, when it was time to sleep, she would ask me for the keys, open the suitcase and put her doll there as well. The dress feels alone at night, she would say, the doll will keep it company. They will talk to each other, and because the suitcase is closed, no one will be disturbed.

*

Can I get you some tea? she asks.

No, it's OK, says Mala.

The mother continues.

On days she wore it, I never had to tell her to be careful so that the dress didn't catch a nail on the wall, I never had to tell her that she should look before she sat down on the grass outside, you must have seen it when you came here, they never clean the lane. But she knew what to do and would return home, the dress exactly as it was when she went out of the house, not one mud stain, not one wrinkle. As if all the while, while her friends were playing, running up and down, she had been standing perfectly still.

Tell me something more about the dress, Mala says.

No, the dress wasn't anything out of the ordinary but, yes, it was a pretty dress, red, cotton, little flowers in front, white and blue. It reached her knees, its sleeves had frills made of lace, white and red. The hooks were in the back, six, all coloured red. Maybe that's why it was special because, usually, you don't get coloured hooks matching with the dress.

Where did you buy it?

Here itself, at the Wednesday fair that's held in the high-school playground. It's on the other side of the market road, away from the hospital where the railway tracks are. Many children go to the fair only to see the trains, she also liked to watch them go by. On fair days, the crowd spills over, people walk very close to the railway line. Once, someone got run over by a train, but that was very long ago, and ever since then, trains slow down when they pass every Wednesday afternoon.

I go there twice every month. Things are expensive these days and we don't have much to spare so I buy very few things, just those I can afford from the money I make every month working in four houses as a maid. Her father is a nice man, he never asks me about that money, how much I get or how much I save.

I make it a point to buy something for her every time I go there. Something small, not very expensive. Like a necklace for three or four rupees, a handkerchief, made of shiny cloth, with little mirrors sewn into it, which she could use as a shawl for her doll, sometimes a pair of glass bangles, a rubber band for her hair.

That day I didn't notice the frock, it was she who pointed it out to me, she tugged at my sari after I had passed Sarkar's shop. Sarkar is the man who has the best stall at the fair since he brings tape recorders, cassettes of film songs, binoculars, packets of playing cards. And because he has these fancy things, everyone respects him, they let him set up his stall in the same place every week, between the two poles that mark the goal in the playground. In winter, while other stalls remain dark or light lamps, Sarkar strings twinkling lights across the poles.

He brings dresses for children only during Durga Puja, but that day he had the red frock and had hung it high above his stall on a bamboo pole for the village to see, like it was a flag or something.

I want the frock, she said. It cost seventy-five rupees,

I told her we would have to wait until next month when Father gets his salary, but she said she wanted it that evening itself.

If you know my daughter, she is the type who never shouts or complains, never asks for anything, she is the perfect child, never once does she cry, sulk, make a face, but that evening when I had walked past the shop, she was behind me, and when I stopped to buy a bar of soap, she kept looking at that red dress which, even from a distance, was as bright and beautiful as when you held it in your hands. I looked at her looking at the dress, I could see her eyes and I knew I had to buy it.

You go get the money, I will wait, said Sarkar, I will bring it down by twenty, he said, just for your little girl.

I had saved about a hundred rupees which I kept in the leather suitcase and I took the notes out, counted fifty-five as she waited outside, and we brought the dress home. In another envelope was the money that my son had sent, that made me feel safe.

The dress fit as if it had been made to her measure. It looked so good that when her father came home that evening and I told her to wear the dress to show, he said we needed to take a picture. The next day, all three of us went to the studio in the market and got a picture taken. I wore the blue sari I had got for the wedding and Father asked for two copies of the photo. He said that next month, the moment he got his salary, he would have the picture framed.

*

The mother pauses, Mala uses that to slip in her questions: What happened that night? Why was she sleeping in the red dress?

And like a cloud, these questions cast a shadow on her face, she tenses, gets up from the floor. Don't ask me anything more, Didi, please go away now, I have already told you so much, the mother says.

No, I won't take much of your time but tell me what do you think happened that night?

You know what, Didi, at times, I think nothing happened. She's very much here, I haven't seen her body, they told me they had cremated her but I think she will come back to me soon, I am waiting for her and that's why I don't close the door. Her father says I am losing my mind but what do I have left to lose now?

Can I see her room, the room where she slept? I will take only one minute.

Please make it quick, she says, I don't want anyone in the house. And she leads Mala indoors, through a door so small that Mala has to stoop to enter the tiny room, its walls freshly painted, a small bed by the window. The light has faded outside so the room is dark. In one corner of the bed, propped up against the wall, Mala can see the girl's doll, handmade. Its face is streaked with mud, its hair made of cloth, torn into strips, painted black but grey where the colour has run, making it seem like an old woman with a baby's face.

Mala leans forward, stretches across and over the bed, picks up the doll, runs her fingers through its hair. From behind her, she can hear the mother crying. She puts the doll back where it was, turns and walks towards the door, stopping for a brief moment to hold the mother's shoulders, wipe her tears away.

Outside, the sky is dark, the same colour she saw from the bus on her way to the town, thick clouds hang low, she wishes again for her umbrella, the walk to the hotel will take at least half an hour, she doesn't want to get drenched. But the clouds in the sky seem to have made up their mind: they will wait for her to reach the hotel.

The hotel room

So the clouds wait, stretched and darkened by water
to a deep grey, trying to keep their weight afloat in the sky
before they burst open, empty themselves onto the earth.
The clouds watch Mala leave the girl's house, they watch
the water fill her eyes but not enough for a drop to roll
out, they watch her adjust the bag, skip over the puddles,
skirt the slush, her eyes fixed on the ground below as she
passes the huge iron gates of the hospital, the market,
where the pavements are clear now, the vegetable sellers
long gone, leaving behind the wooden skeletons of their
stalls into which they will breathe life again tomorrow
morning.

Jute strands from the baskets lying on the road try to
trip her up, shreds of plastic that must have ripped off
the large sheets clap against her feet as her shoes scuff
discarded vegetable peels, hit an over-ripe tomato that's
rolled down the pavement's incline to come and rest in
the drain, a gash on its surface through which its seeds
and pulp dribble out, like pus from a wound.

She takes long strides to clear the large patches of
water where the fishmongers were. Once she looks up at
the sky. The clouds look back at her, they smile, a sliver
of sun glinting through the parting of their lips. Mala

hurries, almost breaks into a jog, her bag flopping on her back with each step that she takes.

But the clouds wait.

They wait for her to walk the entire stretch of the road, turn right into the lane, walk a dozen or more steps until she reaches the entrance of the only hotel in the town, four rooms in two storeys above a restaurant where, at the entrance, they have a huge earthen oven and two iron tubs, almost as big as the ones she saw with the fish in the morning – these must be for cooking the rice and the vegetables.

The clouds wait for her to walk into the restaurant, between the rows of wooden benches and tables, all empty since lunchtime is over. Mala steps into the lobby, closes the glass door behind her, and the moment she's inside, safe and dry, the clouds burst.

It rains in this small town like it's never rained before.

A room, she says.

The front desk is more like a counter at a post office, it has a glass partition smudged with fingerprints, streaked with watermarks, a semi-circular cut-out at its bottom for hands to be pushed through. To pass the money, pick up the receipt.

Looking through the glass, Mala can see a man, about fifty, wearing glasses, bald except for a dozen or so strands of hair stretched tight from one ear to the other, dyed black, clumsily – the dye has made dark blotches on his scalp just above the forehead. In a mirror behind the man, Mala sees herself, her face tired and dark, her metallic earrings dulled by the dust, her hair dry, the shoulders of her shirt streaked with sweat. Her lips are chapped, she wets them with her tongue, there's a scratch on her arm, maybe she scraped against some stone, a brick, when she was walking up the canal trying to hold on to the shifting ground below.

She knows by heart the lines from the post-mortem report: *There is bruising of the lips and tongue. There are multiple abrasions of various sizes and shapes on upper limbs and back of body.*

How many days, Didi? he asks with a smile.

Only one night, she says, I will leave tomorrow morning.

He takes out the register from a place she cannot see, raises it over the glass partition, hands it to her, a ballpoint pen, without its cap, tied to the register with a string that runs down the spine. She fills out her name, returns it to him and he bends down below the counter to get the keys. And in the half minute or so that she sees his back, that he takes to get the keys, she takes out her white handkerchief and rubs her neck, pressing hard beneath her hair. When she looks at the handkerchief, her neck has drawn black lines on the white fabric. She folds it hurriedly as if someone were watching. She needs a bath.

Do you have warm water? she asks.

No, Didi, but I can send you a bucket, give me fifteen minutes, says the man. You can go upstairs this way, he says, pointing towards the flight of stairs, narrow and steep, so steep they have two railings, one on either side to hold as you climb.

It's the second room on the left, it has a small window

that opens to the street. Complete privacy, he says, again with a smile.

Can I help you with the bag?

No, that's OK. Mala walks up, her shoes leave dirt marks on each step.

When she reaches the landing, she sees another man, this one on his knees, scrubbing the floor, a bucket of water by his side, black with the dust. Still bent, the man turns himself to let her pass, doesn't even look at her as she reaches her door.

The room is small, so small it seems they built it with neither a drawing nor a plan. As if they asked someone to play the guest, then they told him to stand by the side of the bed, placed the side table and then built the walls all around. Because the moment Mala enters, she feels the room crowded. In one corner is a small green door that leads to the bathroom where she sees a tiny sink, a bath area – just enough for her to stand – and a toilet, its bowl stained in several places, a bottle of acid by the side. But it's clean, there's no smell, that's all that matters.

She switches the fan on to let the hot, humid air escape, drops her bag on the bed and walks across, four steps, to open the window. The glass panes close on her with a crash, almost catching her fingers. She opens them again, fixes the latch to keep them open and listens to the sound of the rain pouring outside, a sound like the roar of a crowd in a stadium heard on the radio, uninterrupted, neither rising nor falling.

The wind is strong too, Mala feels spray on her face. She closes the window and through its dirty glass she can see, if she strains her eyes, that the rain is getting heavier by the moment, the sky is a dark grey, all the clouds merged into one.

She returns to the bed, lies down, her legs still on the floor, she shakes the slippers off, her heels hurt, a pain shoots up and down and up both her calves. She looks at the fan, at the blur of the blades, the iron hook on the ceiling from which the fan hangs. She closes her eyes.

The girl's mother, she reminded her of her own mother, the same height, the same way of sitting on the floor, with legs drawn up, chin on the knees while listening, both have the same way, nervous and clumsy, of adjusting the sari where it keeps slipping over the shoulder.

She is six years old, it's raining.

Father is standing at the door of the house, ready to go to work, Mala is trying to push him out of the door.

She's small, barely over three feet, her head only reaches his knee. His legs don't move, he leans against the door and looks down at her, runs his fingers through her hair, she keeps pushing, her face set, her lips clenched.

You want me to get wet, he says, let me take my umbrella.

No, no, she shouts, just get out of the house.

Are you listening to your daughter, Father calls out to Mother who is in the kitchen, I have to be in the office early today. He moves ahead with a sudden jerk, Mala's hands slip, she falls down, begins to cry as he walks into the house, picks up the umbrella, stops at the door for a second or so and pokes her in the back with it.

Go play inside, don't be such a cry-baby, he says.

She doesn't get up, she's covered her face with her hands and through her fingers she sees his shadow step over her and walk out, she hears him close the door hard, the sound rings in her ears.

She runs to the balcony, watches him walk to the bus stop while the rain splashes the iron grille. She wipes her eyes and looks towards the kitchen from where she can hear Mother washing dishes, the noise of scrubbing, of ash on steel.

She stands at the kitchen door and Mother turns to look at her.

Go inside and play, Mala, everything's all right, I am here.

The doorbell rings.

Mala hadn't realized the room had a bell but now she can see it, a huge steel clapper, rusted brown, stuck to the wall above the door like some strange insect that's scurried inside the house to escape the rain.

Your hot water is here, Didi. The man who was scrubbing the floor is standing there with a blue bucket, half full. Steam licks his hands. Beside him is the boy she saw at the tea stall, the same boy who was washing the cups and the plates, arranging them on the tray, his shirt wet with rain and sweat. He recognizes her as well, smiles.

Put it in the bathroom, she says.

They both walk across the room, the bucket hits a corner of the bed, the water splashes, a drop falls to the floor, they don't notice.

It's very hot, Didi, you can mix some cold water.

She will not wet her hair, that will take too long a time to dry, so she washes her face and then pours water from the neck down. There's a small cake of new soap on the sink which is meant for washing hands, she should have bought one on her way to the hotel but she uses this one. It doesn't lather, only leaves white lines on her body yet she scrubs hard. She can see her grime flow in dark lines towards the drain. She soaps her neck, behind her ears, her shoulders, sits down to reach her knees, her feet, between her toes.

She walks out, wrapped in a towel. She hasn't walked naked for a long, long time so she lets the towel fall. Her heart races, is someone looking? She looks at the window, it's locked. The door is locked as well but just to be doubly sure she slides the bolt. She lies on the bed, closes her eyes, she's hungry but she will wait until she gets up.

This time, there are no dreams, no images from the past, sudden and sharp, just the sound of the rain outside, drumming the window as she slides into sleep, her bare arm against her bare forehead, her eyelashes brushing the skin above her wrist, her legs on the white bedsheet while the rain continues to pour. Water collects outside, on the streets and in the drains, laps against the bamboo frames of the vegetable stalls, washes away the seeds and the pulp of the over-ripe tomato lying in the drain, fills the tiny yard she saw from Dr Choudhury's chambers, the used syringes float in circles, the water submerges the steps that lead to the hotel lobby, floods the clearing that she walked on, the canal where she stood, covers the five red bricks, wets the cement platform in the post-mortem room.

Post-Mortem Man, what a waste, she thinks; but before she can dwell on it, Mala is asleep.

The dinner and the rain

MALA'S EYES OPEN five hours later to darkness, to the dank smell of the towel where it lies on the floor, rolled up in folds and shadows like a child sleeping, curled up on a street, cold and wet. She can feel a chill across her bare skin, how could she have gone to sleep with nothing on, what if someone had forced open the door? Shivering, she switches on the light, dresses in the only change of clothes she has got and rings the bell. She hasn't had anything to eat the whole day, the hunger thrashes around in her stomach like the mackerel in the aluminium tub she saw this morning, its soapy froth riding right up her chest to her mouth where she feels its bitter taste.

So quiet is everything that the bell keeps ringing in her ears even when she has taken her finger off its switch. Even when she has closed her fist, opened it, her ears still ring, stopping only when she hears hurried steps up the stairs, light and fast – it must be the boy from the tea stall.

What can you get me to eat?

What do you want? he asks, holding one side of her door, raising and lowering his right leg in an impromptu exercise.

Anything hot.

Mother had told her when you eat outside and aren't sure how safe the food is, always ask for piping hot, straight from the stove, the hotter the better since bacteria die in the heat.

Toast and eggs, he says.

And what else?

We have tomato sauce.

Bring it, she says, make it quick, I have to go out.

Yes, Didi, he says, not more than ten minutes. He smiles again, his teeth a flash of lightning in the tiny dark cloud of his face. She can hear his steps down the staircase, two at a time.

Looking out of the window, all she sees is water, as if she were on the deck of a boat. It's still raining but it's a light drizzle now, like in the morning, when she walked through the market. But this time, because of the wind, the drops fly down in curves, set against the light of the only street lamp that's on, the rest all switched off. Some of the rain blows in, sprays her face, but after her bath that only adds to the freshness so she doesn't mind. She sees the reflection of the light in the water-logged street, shifting and jagged, as if an old painter, his hand trembling, has run a brush of yellow paint over the black canvas. She can see the water part around the legs of a man who's rolled his trousers up to his knees, and lap at the folds. Far away, when she bends her head to look, someone has planted a red flag on a stick. There must be an open sewer there, perhaps a manhole with its lid removed so that the water can drain out. In the city, they sometimes do that to warn pedestrians. Especially when a tram wire snaps in the rain, falls down, charges the water with electricity.

She holds her breath for a second, just to hear the water against the walls of the pavements, the edges of houses and shops on either side, the glass door of the hotel. She likes the sounds of the splashes of feet on their way home, the gurgle in a drain, a handcart pusher shouting for others to make way.

She always liked it when it rained so hard. For one, school would be cancelled and she could play the Flood Game with Mother. This meant both of them going to the kitchen, taking stock of whatever there was, taking a piece of paper and drawing up a schedule, in black and red felt-tip pens, of what to do, how much to eat if the rain turned into a flood and they were stranded at home for the next week. They would ration all supplies, one cup of rice instead of the usual two, either a dal or a vegetable but not both. They would divide biscuits into portions, count the crumbs, cut the only bar of soap in the bathroom into pieces, one for each person, one for each day.

The eggs are hot with onions, chopped and fried to a deep brown, the first spoonful almost burns her tongue so she keeps her mouth open, tries to cool it by blowing short breaths.

There are four slices of bread wrapped in tissue paper stained dark with the oil from the eggs. There's a bottle of sauce on the tray, she pours some out, not even looking at the thick red crust that clings to the tip and the cap.

The red sauce spreads on the yellow eggs and the brown onions; the spoon is steel but dull and rusted.

Stomach contains food material (small quantity) including pieces of onion.

Using the spoon, she mixes the eggs with the sauce. The man must have washed the plate and not wiped it dry since there is a film of water at its bottom that has softened the bread to a soggy brown.

The hair easily comes off . . . blood-stained frothing from mouth and nostrils, eyes protruding . . . brain liquefied.

She can't eat. She rushes to the bathroom to rinse her mouth, the water from the tap is a deep red, mixed with black, like the water she saw in the canal. It splashes against the white sink, leaving red streaks. She retches hard but, because she hasn't eaten much, she doesn't throw up anything except a spasm that travels from the base of her stomach to her throat, waters her eyes. Suddenly, as abruptly as it started, it's over; the water runs clear now. She rinses again, drinks a few gulps, likes its coldness settling in her stomach, returns to the bed and lies down. For a moment, she sees the girl's mother standing in her room, crying, holding the doll in her hands, but that image disappears as she closes her eyes and opens them again. That's what happens when you eat after a very long break, her mother had said, your stomach starts to churn, you see all sorts of things in front of your eyes.

Her next stop is the home of the police officer, maybe he can help.

The shadow in the room

MALA LIKES walking in water, she likes its resistance, solid and yet constantly changing, the cool wetness against her calves, sometimes reaching up to her knees, the countless uncertainties that lie beneath. She thinks of them as a shoal of question marks swimming below the surface, in and out between her toes, their hooks teasing, curling around her bare feet. Every step is a surprise, what will she walk into next? A dead leaf that will stick? A sharp pebble that hurts? A pothole in which she will fumble, trip? Will a bus pass by, cut the water in a deep swirl so that she has to stop, let the wave pass before she can go on? Or should she take the wave straight on, let it push her hard so that she loses balance? Should she walk ignoring all this, as if there were no water, like she walks on streets, bending her knee a bit, raising her legs, one splash after another?

No, she settles for an exaggerated walk, a slow drag, her legs fairly straight, rising high, the heels kicking back but only gently. It must look funny, she thinks, like those wind-up dolls walking in shop windows on Park Street. This slows her down but she has time, it's only eight in the evening.

*

She called the superintendent of police, Mr R. K. Bose, from the hotel. You are lucky, he said, that your phone is still working because most lines are dead, I have got several complaints, one even from the district magistrate. Come whenever you can, my home isn't far from where you are, walk down the main street, the one that leads to the hospital via the market, take a turn to the left just before you see the hospital's sign. I am at the end of that street, you will see my jeep parked outside. Let's hope it doesn't drown before you reach here, he laughed.

She liked the voice.

Mala wonders what to wear, maybe the fresh set of clothes she has put on after the bath, but why? Through the window she can see it's still drizzling, the streets are waterlogged, what's the point? I'll get wet again, I have one full day left, tomorrow, and then the journey back to the city, three hours by bus. I should have at least one dry set. She decides to leave the clean, fresh set for tomorrow.

She undresses again, picks up the clothes lying on the floor, the ones she came to the town in, they have dried, more or less. The water's gone, leaving a sediment of smells: from the Post-Mortem Man, the dead marigold flowers, the hyacinths in the canal, the market, the fish in the tubs that sprayed her with their froth. Talcum powder should take care of that, she always carries a small box in her bag, she sprinkles generous amounts on her neck, between her breasts, its sweet yet strong lime smell smothers the others as she slips into the same clothes, the blue jeans and the shirt. There's no one who will notice my clothes at this time anyway, she thinks, it's dark, it's wet, it's late, there will be few people on the street. She can't afford to wet her only pair of shoes, so she decides to walk barefoot.

There's no one in the hotel lobby when she comes downstairs. Two mops lie on the floor, pushed to one side, wet and dripping. She can see the marks they have left on the floor, on the glass door as well: the water dried, the mud still there.

This is the third time today she's walked down the same street and each time it's been different.

From the morning, she recalls the plastic sheets catching the wind, curling over to show her the vegetables, the flash of their colours, the crowd spilling from the houses on either side. On her way back, in the afternoon, the vegetable-sellers had gone, leaving behind torn baskets, rotten peels, the crowd was still there but with different faces, walking at different speeds. And now there's just water.

Almost up to her knees, covering the pavement, lapping against the shuttered storefronts. Candles flicker in some windows, the rain must have knocked down some electricity pole. Two children, a boy and a girl, splash, send a spray of dirty, black water towards her, Mala moves away. She will have to take another bath when she returns.

Her day has almost come to an end, after Mr Bose there's no one she has to meet tonight. She hasn't found much, in fact, nothing to add to the sheet of paper that's still in her bag except details, interesting but trivial. Like the polio charts in the RMO's room at the hospital, the

Post-Mortem Man's knife, hammer and chisel, the two boys and the old woman at the canal, the five stepping stones, the sound of a car or was it a truck above on the highway. Yes, the mother's story of the dress, the doll on the bed, that could mean something, what she doesn't know. But instead of the familiar knot of panic in her stomach, Mala feels confident, a little more assured than earlier, maybe it was the heat and the hunger, one banished by the rain, the other by the food – although she hardly ate any; maybe it's the bath she had that washed all the dirt away. Or perhaps it's just because she likes walking in water.

She is in the lane that leads to the police officer's house, it must be a dirt road since she can feel the ground slip from under her feet. She plays safe, moves to the edge of the lane and with one hand holds the wall that runs on one side. It's dirty, wet, she can feel the rough plaster chipped off in several places, she can read the election graffiti, the white paint of the hammer and the sickle, some candidate's name.

Her toes stub against something but she goes on, the skin on her feet, under water for so long, will have wrinkled for sure. Dr Choudhury had told her once that her skin was very sensitive to water, especially that on her hands and on her feet, she had to stay at home for a full week before she could go back to school.

Suddenly, like light in a dark room, she sees the jeep at the end of the road, white and blue, its wheels under water. That must be the police officer's house. She looks at the stretch she's left to cover – shouldn't take more than five minutes.

Mala is eleven years old, she studies in Class Five. She wakes up in the morning and so overcast is the sky that the bedroom is still dark, Mother has switched on the light in the hallway. On her way to the bathroom, when she looks outside, it's raining like she has never seen before. As if the sky were pouring the rain in buckets, not in drops. It must have started late in the night because the bus stop is under water, its level right up to the iron base of the lamp post.

Mother says there's no point in Mala going to school, Father, as always, says the opposite – how do you know there will be no school? Mala begins to dress in the dark.

After breakfast, when she goes to the sink on the balcony to wash her hands, she has to run pressed against the wall since the rain lashes at her face, her shoulders, the collar of her white shirt which Mother ironed last night.

Father waits at the door with an umbrella, Mala always wanted an umbrella of her own, a small red or white one with flowers, like the other girls in school. But Father says, I have already bought you a raincoat, it has flowers as well, an umbrella is a waste of money. He tells her to take off her shoes, socks, wraps them up in a newspaper and jams the package into her bag, still slung on her back.

The bus is empty, all its windows closed, the conductor's hair plastered to his head as if he just had a bath and didn't dry his hair. Father props his umbrella against the edge of the seat marked for Ladies and Children. Mala sits there, turns her face to look out of the window. Through its narrow glass she can see nothing except the grey blur of more water and some sky.

Whenever it rains hard, her friends in her class bring their own umbrellas. She likes watching as they open them, one by one, line them up in the corridor outside the classroom to dry. Then she plays a little game.

She gets up, asks the teacher for a water break, walks down the corridor and, before going down the stairs to where the water taps are, she stands at the end and looks at the umbrellas. Then she leans her head to one side, rests it on the wet iron railing and stares hard down the corridor, its marble floor. She imagines the floor is a garden with white grass and the brightly coloured umbrellas, all opened out, are flowers, lined up in pools of water below each, the drops that have dripped down the plastic. She keeps staring, unblinking, so hard that within a minute or so her eyes begin to blur, the classrooms and their doors fade away, the entire school seems to bloom with flowers, all in their own little plots, wet and fresh.

School has been called off. Inside the main gate they have put a blackboard in the lobby in front of the principal's office: *Rainy Day, Holiday.*

You stay here, I will pick you up in two hours, I'll take the day off as well, says Father. How could I know that school was closed?

But she doesn't mind, she likes school when it's deserted, its emptiness makes it look different, new, filling her with a sense of adventure. So she leaves her bag by the gate, puts on her shoes, removes her raincoat and walks to her favourite place, where the water taps are. There's no shelter there but she doesn't care. As she bends down to drink, the rain falls on her head, she likes the sound and the feel of the drops drumming her head. Like when Mother oils her hair every Saturday; Sunday is for shampoo.

She goes up the stairs and walks down the corridor outside the classrooms. It's quiet, the only one that's open is Class Six; she walks inside. She stands in front of the class, walks up and down, she's Miss now so she picks up the yellow chalk and writes her name on the blackboard, wipes it away fast with the duster.

There's a measuring scale standing against the wall in one corner, she walks up to it and measures her height: exactly four feet, four inches.

She sits in the teacher's chair and looks at the empty rows in front, climbs down and walks to the other corner. A very beautiful girl sits here, she has long hair that reaches to her waist, she doesn't talk to anybody. Mala goes and sits at her empty desk. There's a plastic wrapper on the chair, she puts it in her pocket, runs her hands over the surface of the desk trying to find out if it's in any way different from her own. Then she hears the shuffle of feet. Heart racing, she runs out of the classroom. It's the sweeper.

Why have you come to school today? he asks.

I didn't know it was closed, she says.

Anyone would have told you that, he says.

Mala looks at the mop in his hand, wet, a bucket in the other full of black water.

It's the worst rain we've had in a long time, I don't know when it will stop, he says. Isn't your father coming to pick you up? he asks.

Yes, he is, she says.

Don't get wet, he says. What's the point in sweeping, mopping up the floor, the rain doesn't stop? I'll do the inside of the classrooms now, the rest later.

She returns to the gate. The guard is there, sitting on his chair, asleep. She eats her tiffin standing there, looking at the blackboard and the rain. Mother had packed sandwiches and potato chips. She always wonders why she can't see the rain as her eyes move higher up, her drawing teacher had said that's because the colour of the rain is almost the same as the colour of the sky so it becomes invisible. If the rain were blue, she said, you could see the drops from as high as you want.

The bus on the way home is so crowded Mala can't see anything; squeezed between two women who are standing, she can see only their stomachs above the saris. Father must be somewhere near the door. When she gets a seat and turns to look, she can see him standing on the footboard, one foot outside the bus, being dragged in the water on the street. Someone tells the conductor please tell the driver to slow down, we don't want water to enter the engine, it will be very difficult to get another bus at this time.

When she reaches home, Mother gives her a towel, her hair is wet, her dress drenched. I told you not to take off your raincoat, Father had shouted at the bus stop, other people were listening, she felt shame, hot in her face, behind her neck. Mala begins to undress, she shivers, looks at the wet pile of clothes on the floor, wraps the towel around her when a shadow enters the room.

She wants to scream but she can't, she doesn't.

For, it's a familiar shadow. And this isn't the first time.

Please come in, Didi, Sir has been waiting for you, says the police constable, leading her to the living room.

There's a towel kept on the chair, please dry yourself, this is the worst rain in a long time, don't know when it will stop, he says.

Mala feels embarrassed, her feet are bare, her jeans rolled up to her knees, she rolls them down, wet and crumpled. The skin around the toes has wrinkled. She covers her legs with the towel, pulls her chair in towards the desk so that no one can see, waits for the police officer, tries to push what she has just remembered back to where it came from.

The police officer

WHY DON'T YOU first dry yourself? Your clothes are wet, your hair is dripping, I'm not worried about the floor or the rug, no, not at all, don't get me wrong, these things can be cleaned up, I have four people to do that, two peons plus two maids, but you may come down with a temperature and if not, at least, a cold. Don't you have an umbrella? You aren't even wearing shoes. Well, I say, who am I to advise today's young people? Do as you wish. Getting back to the point, tell me how I can help you?

His words come in a torrent, thick and fast, so fast that Mala can't make out if here is a man eager to help or just another officer, she knows the type, warming up to unleash a flood of facts that will wash all her questions away, all unanswered.

Mr Bose sits down in the chair. There's a white towel draped on its backrest with a light smudge where his head rests, must be the oil in his hair. He pulls his chair in closer to the desk and draws up a notepad in front of him. As if he were a doctor about to prescribe something.

In fact, he does remind Mala of Dr Choudhury, slightly older, in his fifties, the grey hair brushed right back, strong arms below the sleeves of his white shirt. Where his watch should have been, Mala notices the skin is lighter, in the shape of a dial and a strap.

No, that's OK, she says, your assistant gave me a towel, I'm all right. I came here to find out more about the girl who was found dead in the canal. I want to know what you think of the case.

Yes, that you told me on the phone. What would you like to know? He is pushing her into a corner, Mala tries to wriggle out.

Any progress on the case?

Well, let me tell you this first, whatever I say is off the record, don't quote me, I don't want to get into any trouble, because I know, from experience, over twenty-five years, that whatever you people say in the press, even if you quote me word for word, there's some kind of trick that you know because whatever appears in the paper is what suits you, it's always different from what I said.

I understand, Mala smiles, please don't worry. I will say police sources.

Progress, what progress can you have in this case? We have nothing, no facilities, nothing. Yes, we have a post-mortem room here but what post-mortem? You said you went there this morning, what did you see? A hammer, a chisel, a knife, no electricity, what can you do with all this? Frankly, I wouldn't even look at the report, it's worthless.

The doctor who is in charge comes only once a week. And, then too, he doesn't do anything, signs the form, goes home, leaves everything to that illiterate Post-Mortem Man who walks around the town telling everybody that he's more qualified than the doctor, that he's Forensic Specialist Number One, you met him, didn't you? What did you think?

He talks a lot but he was helpful, says Mala, he showed me some places.

My advice to you is don't take anything he said seriously. What does he know? His father cut bodies, his grandfather did the same thing, now he's training his son to do it. It's in his blood, not in his head. Let me tell you, from the first day I have been telling myself that something is wrong in this case, something doesn't make sense here. Why should this girl be left in the canal? Have you been there, to the canal?

Without waiting for an answer, Mr Bose continues: You walk to the canal and everyone can see you, the road is on top, buses, trucks, cars, all keep going, that's the main highway from the city. Then there are houses on either side, everyone is up until late in the night, watching TV, they have nothing to do here except watch TV, many of them don't even have food to eat at night but they will watch TV. Getting back to the point, my point is they found the body in the evening, before sunset. Someone should have seen whoever it was who dumped the body there. Either that or no one is telling. We have made inquiries but have found nothing, excuse me, would you like some tea? I'll get some, please wait.

Mr Bose gets up, lifts the curtains, walks inside. Mala can hear his voice, a woman's voice too.

She looks around the room. In one corner, there's a

glass showcase with glass shelves. There's a brass Buddha, two ashtrays made of stained glass with coloured pieces, four dolls, all lined up on the shelf. One has leaned to one side, the other three look straight at her. There must be a child in the house, most likely a girl. Mala can make out what looks like a stuffed kangaroo – or is it a deer? – a box of marbles, an incense-stick holder made of brown wood, shaped like a candle with a wide base for the ash to fall and collect.

Sorry for taking so long, what was I saying?

That there was something strange about her being found in the canal.

Yes, that's my point. You see, I believe that you must look at the whole picture, don't go by what's obvious, because the most obvious things aren't always the truth. Let me give you a personal example, I hope I am not wasting your time.

No, please go ahead. What else can Mala say?

Long ago, when I had just entered the service, Mr Bose begins, they posted me in a town in the hills. I was young, like you, full of energy, it was one of my first assignments and I was newly married, I wanted to impress my wife.

This wasn't what we call a crime-prone area. The only major illegal activity was the chopping down of trees by a local mafia who then sold the logs on the black market. One day, I got a call in my office saying that several dozen trees, prime teak, have been chopped in the night and taken away via the national highway. I wasted no time, alerted every police station along the way, informed head-quarters. They sealed the border, they put roadblocks up, but no sign of the loot, the truck, nothing.

There was also no accident on the way – the road there is very narrow, have you been there? If you haven't, my advice is please go. It's beautiful, cedar trees line the road and that road turns and twists in hairpin bends. On one side are the hills, on the other is a gorge, at the bottom of which is the river, its water pure and fresh. These days they talk of mineral water from the hills in bottles. When I was there, I would drink straight from the river, I had no health problems.

Getting back to the point, we searched far and wide and then gave up. After all, we had a limited staff and there were other problems. They were having municipal elections, I think, and so all of us were put on election duty.

We all forgot about the case. But one day, a few months after the incident, I was sitting in my living room, it was a Sunday and I was relaxing after a hard week. My eyes fell on a chair, a new chair that my wife had bought from the local market and she said she bought it at a very cheap price, about two hundred rupees or something. And then it struck me, this was the answer.

That same evening, I took three constables, went to the market, rounded up the furniture man and all his staff. He led us to his house, and guess what we saw. In his backyard, logs and logs of wood. So this was the man who was doing it, chopping the trees, stealing the wood, taking it just a couple of miles away, using it to make chairs and tables, bookcases, right under our noses while we were guarding the border. And selling it to people around, imagine selling it even to a police officer's wife.

My wife, I tell you, she wasn't happy at this. She liked the chair a great deal but stolen property is stolen property. We had to seize the chair, but think of it, if I hadn't noticed it, nothing would have happened, the looting would have gone on and on.

The constable enters with a tray with two cups of tea. Mala likes the warmth of the glass against her fingers.

See, that's what I mean, you look at facts, you draw the first pattern the facts make and then you stick to that pattern even if it's wrong. That's the problem. The truth, I have often found, lies somewhere else, it's linked to the facts but outside the pattern. That's why I'm glad you are meeting all kinds of people here. You may not get any answers – in fact, I'll be surprised if you find out more than what we have – but no harm in looking, I say. Look, look wherever you can look.

An hour has passed, Mala keeps trying to nudge him back. But every time she has a specific question, he goes off on a tangent so sweeping that she cannot but let him speak, wait for the pauses to slip the question again.

This time, he gets up and walks into the house, comes back with a tray of biscuits. Have these while you are here, having tea on an empty stomach isn't a good thing. These are her favourite biscuits, the ones with the cream filling.

Wasn't the girl found in the canal? Mala asks, using the silence as he eats a biscuit.

That's my point, he says, his mouth half full. Aren't

you listening, my question is why will her body be left in the canal? Getting back to the point, between you and I, there is no genuine investigation in these cases. The girl's family couldn't care, they don't have a mouth to feed, the father works in the city, he comes to visit them once a month, the mother is a maid, she is in shock, I hear, but don't worry. These people are tough, I have found that in small towns, they recover faster than we do.

The post-mortem report says there were multiple abrasions of various sizes, Mala says, she knows the lines by heart. A handkerchief was also found in her mouth and she was strangled.

You can't be sure of that. Frankly, I am not sure of any post-mortem here. You see, I was in the city when they called me. It was too late, otherwise I would have sent the body to the district hospital, they take things a bit more seriously than we do. The young doctor who supervised the post-mortem is a nice chap but I don't think he asked the right questions. My hunch is, he had some facts, he drew a pattern and never looked out. The Post-Mortem Man must have told him half of the stuff and he made it out to be an open-and-shut case. In fact, he was in such a hurry that he didn't even wait for me to return. He discharged the body, handed it over to some relative, not even the father.

What about the rape? The report says there were signs of sexual assault.

These things happen in north India, where some think that if you have sex with a child, you get cured of your disease. You must have read about it, but in these parts we don't have that at all. People are much more cultured, so I think the injuries were caused when she fell down the canal, maybe some stones or something.

A girl enters the room.

Say hello to Mala Didi, she is a reporter from a newspaper, Mr Bose tells her. This is my daughter Mira, very bright. She comes first in her class. And before Mala can exchange any word with her he says, now you go inside, do your homework.

Mala smiles at the girl who smiles back and walks inside.

So are you looking for anyone? Will there be any arrests?

See, my theory is simple: I think she went to play there and slipped, that canal is dangerous. I have been telling the district magistrate please do something, not only is it a breeding ground for malaria but in the summer we have enteric diseases as well, but he keeps saying, Mr Bose, we have no funds. I say, how much will it take? Pour bleach, clean it up, remove everything, plant some nice trees or something, even Mira could go there once in a while. Now she has nothing to do, she can't play in the canal with maids' children. So she goes to school and comes straight back, there's not even a park here I can take her to.

I love the city, I was born there, lived there up to my college days; and since then, I have been touring the state, one town after the other, catching criminals, that's my job. But if you ask me, where will you settle after retirement – I have a few years to go – I will say not to any town or a village but the city.

I read, I think it was in your paper, they are going to

build a very tall building in the Maidan called Paradise
Park. I can't understand what all this hullabaloo is about.
When there is no development, newspapers say dying city
dying city; when they plan to build something ultra-
modern, they say that's not a good thing.

Getting back to the point, if you need a quote, you
can write this: The police are investigating the case. A
massive manhunt has been launched for two suspects.

Who are these suspects? Mala asks.

That's for the quote, Miss Mala, Mr Bose smiles as he
gets up. My constable will drop you at the hotel.

No, that won't be necessary.

I know nothing is necessary but how will you go back?
It's very late and it will take him only a few minutes. Call
me if you have any other questions. Or call me if you find
something that you think will be of help to us. This case
isn't so important, it's bottom priority for us, but if you
find something, let us know. And nothing on quote, please.

The constable wades across the water, starts the jeep
and pulls up right in front of the house. Mala gets into
the front seat and Mr Bose closes the door as the jeep
starts. Its wheels spin, lurch forward, churning the water.

Tomorrow morning, they will open all the drains, the
constable says, I have been here four years and this is
the worst. Didi, you got your work done?

Yes, Mala says.

Some people have come out of their homes after dinner
and are standing in clusters. They give way for the jeep to
pass, some of them look inside, look at her as she clutches
her bag close, feels the floor mat in front underneath her
bare feet, the cigarette stubs, ash and mud.

Mala rests her head against the window. She closes her eyes. All she can recall of the meeting with Mr Bose is his daughter, her face as he said you go inside do your homework, the four dolls in the showcase, the one that leaned to one side.

Didi, here's your hotel, says the constable.

Thank you, she says, offers him a tip, which he refuses.

I am on duty, he says, smiles, starts the jeep.

Mala waits until it turns around the corner leaving behind a white wake in the black water, then she turns to enter the hotel.

Waiting for Alam

MALA WAKES UP what she thinks is hours later but her watch says it's been only fifteen minutes – has it stopped? She remembers the raindrops on the dial, water could have got in but no, the second hand is moving. It's just after midnight. Light from the hotel hallway squeezes in through her door in a thin, bright line, so she pulls the covers over her to trap what she can of the night, closes her eyes and watches her head begin to grow.

The rest of her remains unchanged, normal, but her head spreads out, on either side, covering the pillow, spilling over, spreading to take up more than half of the bed so that her hair now touches the floor. The head covers the entire bed now, growing and growing, until she can feel the floor cold against her neck, the walls press against her ears, her forehead scrapes the ceiling. She raises her hands to her face but she can't, they are too small to reach anywhere. Then, in her room-sized head, she sees a darkness; her eyelids part like curtains in a movie theatre on which scenes begin to play out in gigantic frames with neither shape nor colour, just a fast blur of black, white and grey, some strains of sound. She sees the tea-stall owner near the bus stop, but instead of taking sugar from the plastic jar behind him, he picks up the little boy, drops him into the huge kettle. His scream mixes with the hiss of the steam that rises, blue and yellow, his tears condense against her glass. She's back on the main market street, the vegetable-sellers look at her, laugh, the children going to school in raincoats stop, one of them hands her an umbrella, a white umbrella with red and blue flowers, says this is the one you always wanted, didn't you, and with the umbrella in her hand she climbs the cement platform where the Post-Mortem Man is waiting, his back towards her. She can hear him wash the hammer and the chisel in the brick vat. Didi, this won't take long, don't worry, he says, I know how to do it, my grandfather did it, my father, even my son knows, it's in my blood not in my head, we won't hurt you. He begins to undress her and at the window she can see her father, smiling, the police officer's daughter comes running in, she tries to snatch the knife away from the Post-Mortem Man while water floods the room, laps against her sides. Her head has grown so big it squeezes itself out of the window and continues to grow, over the street, down the lanes, over the water, to the bus stop.

She wakes up, it's been only ten minutes since she closed her eyes.

What's happening? she wonders. Ever since the morning she has been getting these flashes, some from the past, some from the present, some from God knows where. I need to get myself together, I have just one more day here, Mala tells herself, gets up, switches the lights on.

From outside, she can hear a splash in the water, someone must be walking by. She goes to the sink in the bathroom to wash her face. There's no water in the tap but there are two buckets full, one cold, the other still warm. They must have put them there just before she arrived back at the room. She splashes water into her eyes, they hurt. She comes back to her room, picks up the bag from the floor and takes out the post-mortem report.

She begins reading it, this time with a pen in her hand, trying to underline what she has to do next.

Body found in canal, yes, she has been there, she marks it with a tick.

Body brought and identified by – the name is illegible, she needs to find that out tomorrow.

Length of body: four feet four inches, she's five feet six, the girl would have reached up to her chest if she were sleeping beside her, on the bed.

She hears a noise.

Pen in hand, poised over the paper, lying on her stomach, her face half-resting on the pillow, she hears the noise. Perhaps it's a cricket or a cockroach chirping, from either outside or somewhere in the bathroom. A door opens in the hallway, maybe some other guest on his way out or in.

She goes back to the report, but there's nothing to add. What did the police officer say? His first job in the hilltown, the man who chopped the trees down, brought them to his furniture shop so that no one would notice. Look at what's not obvious, he had said, what's not written. Well, all she has seen or heard today is in a way what's not written but she is nowhere closer to the answer.

The lights go off, there's a power cut.

Generator available, read the sign on the door in the

lobby, but she isn't sure anyone is awake now to know that the power has gone. And anyway, it isn't so hot, the wind is cool. She opens the window to let the draft in and then lies down on the bed, closes her eyes again.

The noise has gone.

Sleep comes, bringing with it her last dream in this small town.

Mala is nine or ten, there's a power cut at home, it's so hot that both Mala and her mother go to the terrace with a thin bedsheet.

We'll spread this out and lie down, Mother says, there's usually a breeze on the terrace.

The only problem is the rough cement surface, which hurts their backs. Mala complains but Mother says we can't do much, just lift the bedsheet, brush away the stone chips that are big and small, make it as smooth as you can and close your eyes. Once you fall asleep you won't feel anything.

Don't be like the princess in that fairy tale, she says, the princess who couldn't sleep on the huge mattress because there was a little pea below.

Mother has been up since morning, washing dishes, packing her tiffin, ironing her clothes, Father's clothes, cooking lunch, cleaning, mopping, washing dishes again, preparing dinner, so the moment she lies down she falls asleep without even waiting for her eyes to close. Or for the much-promised wind to blow.

Mala lies down as well, feeling the heat from her mother radiate in waves. She looks at the stars, the moon, an aircraft go by. Father has told her that at this height in the sky, it's the international air corridor. And at this time, these are aircraft going to England, America from Japan, China – and they pass right over our house. He isn't home yet. He works at the newspaper, his night shift usually ends by midnight but he has told Mother some nights I will be late, don't ask me why, news happens all the time.

Mala gets up and walks to the edge of the terrace. She watches the road below, the houses on either side. One house has a generator, that family also has a car and a dog, and whenever there's a power cut, within three to four minutes, every one in the neighbourhood hears the crank of their generator and all their lights come on.

Mother asked Father one day how much a generator costs and he laughed, she never mentioned the generator again.

After walking around the terrace for a few minutes, Mala knows this is a long power cut. She can make out when it's a short one, when it's a long one. If everything's off, even the street lights, you know there's some hope because they can't have so much blackness sitting around for so long a time. But this is one of those unfair power cuts when one side of the neighbourhood has all the lights. This means either the voltage has tripped or one phase has blown or there's something wrong with the transformer.

She has flicked all the switches on, those for the lights and the fans, so that when the power is back, she will know. Because from the terrace, lying down, she will see light spill out of the rooms below, get reflected back to the terrace, she will see the iron railing glint.

She hears the sound of a car door closing. Father must

be back. She puts her hand over her eyes, pretends she's asleep. He climbs up the stairs and steps out onto the terrace. She sees him walk to the edge, light a cigarette, she hears the match being struck, his breath as he exhales. He walks to where they are sleeping – she shuts her eyes again – and he sits down beside Mother but then gets up almost immediately, walks down the stairs, leaving behind a tiny cloud of smoke that takes a while to disappear since the wind is yet to blow.

Hours later, Mala wakes up. It's still dark but all the street lights are now on, the power is back, she is about to wake Mother up, tell her let's go downstairs, when she realizes that the house is still dark.

She walks down the stairs, she can hear the fan in the bedroom, the sound it makes where a wire has come loose, and then she understands what's happened. Father watched them sleep, he watched them drenched in their pools of sweat, and when the power came back, instead of asking them to come down and join him, he switched off all the lights and the fans so that, sleeping on the terrace, they would not know. Except, of course, the one fan he needed.

Mala is angry and afraid.

She quietly walks back to the terrace where Mother sleeps, lying on her side now, her tired shoulder rising and falling, her blouse now so wet with sweat that it seems she's been drenched in hot rain. She waits for the morning.

She wakes up, there's the noise again.

No, it isn't a noise, it's a shape. Silent and still, sitting in the chair near the window, more like a shapeless shape in the dark.

Is it her clothes, her bag? Is it the shape of the towel she used to dry herself after the bath, dank, rolled up into a ball?

And then that grey blur moves, imperceptibly, but enough for her to know that someone's there, man, woman, child, boy, girl she isn't sure, all she can make out is someone very very thin.

She closes her eyes once, opens them again. Yes, it's better now, clearer, she can see the bag and the towel lying on the floor, the shape takes a form in the chair. The form of someone, a person.

I can help you, he says, my name is Alam.

Alam

HER HEART should race in fear, her lips should dry, her voice should either break into a scream or freeze into a silent chill; if she can get some courage and a few words, she should ask who are you? How can you take my name, turn it around, make it yours? What do you mean, I can help you? How did you enter my room? Why shouldn't I scream, alert everyone in this hotel? But Mala doesn't say all this.

She says, how long have you been sitting here?

Alam doesn't say anything, he gets up, walks across the tiny room to her bed, his strides are small, Mala can count him take five steps, it takes her three from the window to the bed.

He stands at the bedside but doesn't look at her. Instead, his eyes are fixed on the wet bundles on the floor, her bag, her clothes, the towel.

She looks at him carefully, he reminds her of all the men she has met this morning, in the town and in her dreams. He has Dr Choudhury's hair, grey and brushed back; the police officer's hands, hairless; the little boy's smile, a flash of lightning in the dark. The bald patch on his head is like that of the hotel receptionist downstairs, the skin around his elbows matches that of the

Post-Mortem Man. Isn't his slouch that of the sweeper at the school? His glasses, like her father's, thin-rimmed, a large gap between the lenses and the eyes? And yet he is someone new.

It's as if right through the day, Alam has been forming himself, bit by bit, picking up features, this from here, that from there, adding some of his own like the ears, small and flared, his height, a few inches taller than hers, his walk, slow. Or maybe he's not ready, fully formed yet, for Mala expects him to change any moment.

You must be tired, he says. You have been walking around the whole day, across the town and back. You haven't had enough to eat, I would say you have had nothing to eat. Just that silly thing the hotel gave you and a piece of that biscuit.

His words come, effortless, slow, with pauses in between where there should not be any. His voice has a distant tone as if he were speaking from some place far away and Mala were only listening in, eavesdropping on a conversation that wasn't meant for her. But his choice of words, especially 'I would say' and 'silly', betray a confidence and concern that to her seem unusual but at the same time entirely appropriate.

Have you had anything to eat, Mala hears herself asking, the covers pulled over her but now she's half-sitting on the bed, her back propped against the pillow, her knees drawn up.

I have, he says.

And then there's silence again, and the power is back, the bedside lamp switches itself on. Alam leaves no shadow, his feet hardly make a noise as he returns to the window, it seems to her that he's gliding along the floor, in and out of the tiny spaces between the bed and the table, the table and the chair.

The light doesn't reach as far as the window, so Alam, for a moment, seems to disappear in the dark, back to that shape in the chair. But Mala has seen him up close, her eyes have taken his picture, etched it in her mind so that now she can look at the shape and make out the details: his legs resting on the floor, his slender hands on the armrest, the wrist at the edge, his face turned away from her. There's a slight beard on his chin, more like a stubble as if he hasn't shaved for a few days; his shirt is blue, the trousers black, held in place by a big belt with a brass buckle.

He looks out of the window as if nothing that happened during the previous five minutes ever happened, as if her room isn't her room but a stop, a railway station or a bus terminus, a public place, where no one, however new or strange, is an intruder, where Alam has stopped for a while and is waiting, letting the world around him pass, fade away.

Where have you come from? Mala asks, her feet now on the floor.

He says something.

Sorry, I didn't get it, she says, but he doesn't repeat it, maybe he didn't hear.

Mala can sense he's distracted, that he's carrying something big and heavy, stretching and straining, and that any question seems like an unwelcome tug, an attempt to stall his journey to wherever he is going.

Who are you? she asks. And then, after a pause, adds: I need to know who you are.

Who are you? he says.

Mala isn't sure if this is a question. Or he's just repeating what she said.

She waits, assumes it's the former and tells him why she's here in the hotel room, what brought her here, the dead girl in the canal, her mother. She tells him how she spent the day searching for answers in what now seem to be all the wrong places. She speaks for a long time, long enough for her to start feeling uncomfortable that he isn't interrupting, interjecting, that he listens without the faintest flicker of reaction on his face.

Maybe he isn't listening at all, maybe he knows it all. Otherwise, how could he have said what he said in the very beginning, about her not eating anything, the silly thing the hotel gave you and the piece of that biscuit. Maybe he's been with her all the while.

You said you could help me, she says.

Yes, he says. This time she hears him, clearly. But you sleep now, you are tired. I will wait.

Before she can ask him anything else, he gets up, and as noiselessly as he had entered the room, he leaves, walks across, opens the door, there's not even the slightest creak. He closes the door behind him. Mala strains her ears to catch something, the sound of his footsteps to the left or the right. Or even down the stairs. But there's nothing, the silence is back, all she can hear is the pane rattling again.

In the bathroom there's a fresh bucket of hot water, she's not sure who brought it. She mixes it with the cold, undresses, pours the entire bucket over herself in one go.

Her hands hurt lifting the bucket but it's worth the effort: she likes the gush and the tumble of the water, all at one time, falling over her, drenching her head, her hair. She keeps her eyes open so she can see the water in front. She likes the sound, like that of the sea in a seashell she pressed to her ear that summer when she went with her family to the Bay of Bengal and watched the crabs, washed up by the waves, trying to hang on to the shifting sand below, the seagulls flying in low circles over the water.

Her bag's back on the table, her clothes folded, neatly, Alam must have done this when she wasn't looking, she doesn't know what to make of it but then decides to let it pass, sleep sits heavy on her eyes.

She cannot push the feeling away that she knows Alam. From someplace and sometime. Where and when she doesn't know but she has seen him, not once but several times. For what else can explain this: here she is, going to bed moments after a total stranger walks into her room, sits in her chair, gets up, walks to her bed, says he wants to help her, tells her to go to sleep and, while she is not looking, picks up her bag from the floor, neatly folds her clothes. But however hard she tries, she cannot place this missing piece. Instead, the jigsaw seems to grow and grow.

And together with the other puzzle of the girl found dead, the pieces multiply, like cells in the body, scatter themselves across a giant floor in her head, millions of them, coloured and jagged, black and white and smooth, all falling into place in a perfect fit sometime in the future, but now, just one maddening mess.

She can see Alam sitting like a child among the pieces,

picking them up one by one, looking at each, putting each down. She wants to see what he does, how the puzzle takes shape, but her eyes are closing now.

And for the first time since she arrived in this small town this morning, Mala sleeps the sleep of angels. Dreamless, full of quiet.

The wedding band

ARE YOU READY, he says, the same voice, distant and soft, the same perceptible pause between each word and, as always, the question mark at the end left unsaid. Alam is standing at the door, the light from the hallway outside passing through him as if he were made of glass. She is ready, she slept for just a few hours, it's still dark outside but she feels light and fresh as if she slept the entire day and night. The heaviness in her head is gone, the countless pieces of the jigsaw puzzle still scrambled but neater, more orderly, as if while she was sleeping, they picked themselves up, gathered in one tidy corner.

Mala has changed into her fresh set of clothes. She has packed everything else in the bag, and as she bends down to pick it up, he says, you don't need your bag, you can come back and pick it up on your way home.

She walks down the stairs two steps at a time, Alam walks step by step. Standing on each with his two feet before taking the next one, like a child who needs to be sure that there's a step below before he can put his foot forward, a sense of caution that helps Mala abandon her own.

Let's go, Alam says.

Where are we going?

I have to show you something.

She follows him, looking closely at his legs, his shoes black, with steel buckles that clink with each step he takes. There is a light wind. She tucks her hair behind her ear, and as her fingers brush her face, she can feel the grime has gone. She can smell the talcum powder on her neck, on her hands.

Alam stops, motions to her with his hand to stop as well. The clink of the buckles, the sound of their shoes, falls silent.

Can you hear it? he says.

Yes, she can hear, from a place not far away, the sound of what seems like some kind of music. No, not a radio, this is no symphony, no sequence of notes carefully planned and played, but a clatter. Harsh and grating. As they walk towards it, Mala can begin to make out something like a trumpet or a saxophone playing a song from a movie she knows but cannot quite recall. Another trumpet joins in, shrill and high-pitched; a third begins to drone in the background; someone plays a drum. The noise gets louder and louder and now they can see a bright white light at the end of the road.

It's a Petromax lamp, carried by a man on his shoulders, and into its light, out of the shadows on either side, walking in half-steps, six men slip out, all dressed in white, all in line, the one who leads the way holding aloft a banner in red silk stitched onto a rectangular piece of blue velvet. Once they emerge from the lane, the man holding the lamp stops, sets it down. The musicians gather around the light, playing their instruments, waiting for someone to appear.

Mala and Alam move over to one side of the street.

Let's wait and watch, says Alam, his voice rising above the noise.

Seeing them, the band stops for a while, one of the musicians looks at Mala, smiles at her. What to do, he says, the saxophone in one hand, this is the time they fixed for the wedding.

Mala smiles. And the band strikes up another tune.

Each of them wears a cap with a feather, all six have six different colours. Their shirts have epaulettes like soldiers have, shoulders with frilly pads stitched on, made of satin and velvet. The noise begins to resemble some kind of music now, as if each harsh note, after leaving each instrument, is being wrapped in the darkness of the dawn, as if the night were a cotton wool muffling the noise, letting the music through.

Other people walk out of the lane, they must be relatives of the bride or the groom, all wearing new clothes. The men have perfectly ironed trousers, shoes newly polished, long-sleeved shirts, two of them even have ties. Two women join them, both in saris that glitter, the lamp's white light bouncing off the tiny mirrors stitched into the fabric.

A child darts out with a fire-fountain, puts it on the street, strikes a match to light it.

Careful, one of the men says to the women, stay away, your saris shouldn't catch any sparks. The women laugh.

The band gets louder as the fire-fountain crackles, gushes fire – blue, white, yellow, red, the flames all concentrated in one intense jet at the nozzle which then rises more than twelve feet in the sky and then comes down in a million sparklers each one of them reflected in the rain on the street. When it's over, a yellow flame leaps out of the fire-fountain, and one of the musicians, still playing his trumpet, kicks it across the street where it extinguishes as soon as it flips over, hits a puddle. Through all the noise, Mala can hear the hiss of fire meeting water.

Where the lane meets the road, there's a house, brightly lit, decorated with coloured streamers and arches over a passageway that's been created with cloth stretched across bamboo poles. Parked in front is a white car decked with flowers, lines of jasmine and hibiscus, the driver dozing at the wheel.

The fountain burnt, the child is back with a sputtering sparkler in one hand, a Catherine wheel in the other, which he puts on the ground, lights, sends it spinning, sparks flying, blue, white and red, in ever-widening circles. The women laugh like children, walk back several steps, hitch their saris to their ankles to avoid the sparks, while the child jumps up and down.

The groom is a man of medium height, medium complexion, his face one of those faceless faces that Mala knows she will not remember again. He is wearing a silk shirt and trousers, the white tassels of his wedding cap half-cover his face.

The bride follows him. Mala is standing near the crowd of relatives who have all come out of the house, men, women and children, all peering over each other's shoulders for one last look at the couple. The driver is now alert, he puts the keys in the car, starts it, waits. The bride is Mala's height. When she passes by, Mala can smell the flowers in her hair. She gets into the car and reaches out to close the door and Mala can see her bangles, gold, the henna patterns on her palms, fingers, bright red.

And in that brief moment, maybe ten seconds or so, between the time the bride closes the door and the car begins to move, Mala goes back nine, ten, eleven years.

To that afternoon at home where her mother says they have liked your picture, they are coming to see you in the evening, go and dress up. He's a good boy, she says, you will like him, he likes you, that's what his father said in the letter. By now, her resistance has all but died, so often she has gone through the motions, so often has she heard that line, they liked your picture, they are coming to see you in the evening.

The man who she will marry sits in the living-room chair, his parents by his side as she brings the tea. What do you want to do after marriage, he asks.

Mother answers for her, she wants to be a reporter like her father to which his mother says yes, that's a good way of remembering your father who died so young but there are so many other things she can do, taking care of the house, my son, her children. Mala passes him the teacup, and when he takes it from her, his fingers touch hers beneath the saucer. She can feel Father's hand touching her, cold, wet. She shivers.

Lying in bed that night, Mother asks do you like him, and she doesn't know what to say. Yes or no, there can be only one answer, Mother says. But Mala has a third, I don't know.

I agree, Mother says, how can you know a person in

two hours, that's why you need to get married, know him for the rest of your life. I am getting very old now, I can die any day, I can't take care of you for ever, you need a man of your own.

The car begins to move, the bride's mother walks with the car, leaning, saying something to her daughter, the car picks up speed, turns into the street, the band gets louder, the child is lighting another fire-fountain, the car waits for the sparklers to die, Mala can see the bride in the back seat looking outside through one window, the groom through the other.

Then the car and the band have gone. The bride's mother is standing in the passageway looking at the empty street, at the two flowers that have fallen off the car as it turned. She picks them up and walks inside.

Let's go, Alam says, I have to show you something.

The new day is still as black as night as they turn into the street that goes via the market. The wooden benches are stacked on the pavement, one on top of the other, waiting to be brought down, disentangled and then lined up for the wicker baskets and their fresh vegetables. The streets are still flooded here. Although the water is down to their ankles, Mala and Alam walk a considerable distance apart to avoid splashing each other. She knows this street very well, the barred stores, the places where the vegetables were, where the fishmongers sat, she passes the spot where one of them called out to her, the old man with glasses tied with a string and it's then that one piece of the puzzle in her head falls into place. Yes, this is where she saw Alam for the first time.

When she walked in the market of her dream, with the harsh white light from the rafters above, when she saw the light dim, the wet entrails on the floor, the corpses being cut, their heads piled up on one side. It was then, she remembers, that she tried to run, and when she reached the end, she had slipped, her feet had lost balance on the slippery surface and it was Alam who had reached out his hand for her to hold, to steady her, and when she regained her footing, he was gone.

And then again at her father's funeral, which she remembered when she was with the Post-Mortem Man, when she stood on the balcony of her house trying to cry but couldn't, he was the one who had lifted her gently so that she could see her mother cry and that made her shed tears as well. Wasn't he also in the school as well, when she waited for Father to pick her up, when she was playing the teacher in the empty class, scribbling on the black-board, walking up and down, looking at the empty rows in front, wasn't it Alam who sat in one corner and alerted her that the sweeper was coming, that she should be careful?

And wasn't it Alam, yes it was Alam, who was there in the room that afternoon when she came back from school, drenched, it was a rainy day holiday. Mother was in the kitchen warming her lunch, while she took off her wet clothes, a pile on the floor, began to dry herself with a towel, big, heavy and white, when the shadow entered, the familiar shadow, big, heavy and dark, and when it left the room, when she began to cry, Alam it was who stood beside her, his hand on her shoulder, his face turned the other way as she put on her clothes, one by one, his fingers wiping away her tears. Alam, who had taken her name, turned it around and made it his own, a man always by her side – a friend.

As he is now, walking in the water, the puddles splashing, leaving streaks on his black trousers.

No, it's all in my head, Mala tells herself, this man in front is a stranger I have met only hours ago.

Let's see what he has to show.

Returning to the canal

HALF-MUD, half-slush is now full water. Yesterday, this was a narrow clearing between two rows of houses, today it's the other way around: the houses are the clearing between vast sheets of water – narrow strips of mud, brick and concrete that seem to have dropped from the sky to land with a splash in this expanse, slow and sluggish, flowing, not flowing; black in the last light of the night.

Mala hesitates, she has her shoes on, should she walk in the water? What about the clean clothes she's wearing, the jeans and the white shirt? They will get wet.

Alam doesn't even stop to look, to get a picture of what lies ahead, he doesn't even roll up his trousers or take off his shoes, he wades in as if he knows what lies beneath.

So Mala steps in as well.

Her shoes help, they guard her bare feet from the submerged objects, the waste of houses on either side, asleep and undisturbed under the water's cover.

Move to one side, Alam calls out, the ground there is firmer, the water more shallow, you can also hold on to the walls.

He has moved to the left; she moves to the right.

She can hear the wedding band, its music, the women

laughing. It can't be, the band has left, this is the noise ringing in her ears. A moment later it's silent, all she can hear is a drip here, a gurgle there, water finding its own level, its own places to hide and seek. And their footsteps, gentle splashes like two boats being rowed, along with the water lapping against the sides of the houses, the little waves that her walking is making, the ripples, green and black, that start from her and travel outwards, in circles, irregular and concentric. A cricket chirps, it must have found a dry place she cannot see, maybe some crevice in some wall.

All the doors around her are locked, the windows shuttered. On one balcony, two floors high, she can see, through the crack in the railing, a family asleep. Soon, these houses will wake up. People will open their windows, look out at the water, come up with ways to cross. Some will drop stones, some will stand in the middle, open a drain, plant a flag to warn other people. Others will just wait inside their houses, wet and dank, for the sun to come out and take some of the water back into the sky.

It's the clothesline, the blue nylon cord.

In the dark, with water all around, Mala wouldn't have been able to make out the girl's house had it not been for the blue nylon cord, the clothesline hanging in the yard. For this is where she stopped yesterday afternoon, on her way back from the canal; this is where she saw the old woman sweeping the floor, stooped, bent underneath the clothesline, the wet towels and the shirts rubbing her back. This is where she had asked. Mala can see the broom, the same broom the old woman had, lying in one corner, leaning against a door that's closed.

There is the house, Mala says.

Alam stops, points to the red-brick house across from the old woman's. Yes, he says, this is the house you visited, where the mother told you about the red dress. We will stop on our way back, everyone must be sleeping now, Alam says. Let's walk to the canal.

By now her legs hurt, her shoes are full of water, she can feel something squeeze its way inside through the narrow gap between her shoes and her ankles to sit between her toes, slimy, wet and cold. Is it alive? she fears. A leech, they live in water, she knows, they suck blood. She moves her toes but that thing is still there, she presses her toes hard against the inside of the shoe, must be a dead leaf or a plant. And then as suddenly as it came, her fear vanishes, the water all around her begins to drain as if some bottomless hole has been opened not far away, a huge pump inside switched on.

They are on hard ground, they are at the edge of the canal, the water is behind them now.

The face in the water

IS THIS THE CANAL? No, it can't be. They must have come to the wrong place, she thinks. She was here less than twelve hours ago, stepping on the five red bricks dropped in an ankle-deep pool of water, amid the clumps of grass and earth, the placid pool of water hyacinth, the highway above her, watching a boy play with a bicycle tyre. And now, instead of the canal, there seems to be a river in spate, green and black, water wherever she can see, roiling and churning; where there was an embankment, hard and unbroken, the one she held on to as she walked up that afternoon, there's now a black line with deep gashes where the earth has given way, fallen into the water.

Mala reaches out for Alam's hand, closes her eyes, opens them again.

Alam is still, his face calm, looking beyond the canal. Her eyes follow his and there it is, a faint light in the horizon – it's morning, the first light of day.

Where were you standing, show me the place? Alam asks.

I can't, she says, I can't make out anything.

What was around you, do you remember?

She remembers, yes, she had heard a bus or was it a

truck pass by above her, she remembers a clearing at the
top through which she had seen the road.

They walk several steps to the right, there is a clearing
right in front.

Maybe that's the one, Alam says, but when they reach
there, there's more water.

Let's walk down, carefully, as far as we can go. I will
walk in front. We need to see the spot where the girl was
found, I have something to show you there, he says.

He leads, she follows, holding his hand, the dawn light
pressed flat between their bodies.

Look ahead and follow me, he says, I will tell you
when to look below.

Alam walks as if he's walking on a hard road, his steps
sure and measured, even graceful. She can see the back of
his blue shirt, the stains the water has left behind, maybe
it's his sweat but she smells nothing. He has said don't
look below, keep looking ahead. Over his shoulders, the
sky is now a pale blue that lights his hair, his ears, touches
her fingers as well.

It's all right, Alam says, don't be afraid, now you can
look below.

He moves away to stand behind her, still holding her
hand. She bends down. There is a face in the water.

The flowing water is a mirror moving ceaselessly, cracking
into ripples, eddies and swirls that form, break and form
again but her reflection itself is frozen. As if it were firmly
anchored, deep down to some huge immovable surface.

Remember what was there in the post-mortem report,

says Alam. She turns to look at him but he says, no, don't look at me, look down below.

Yes, she knows all the lines by heart, their exact sequence, their short words sometimes not even making a complete sentence, irregular, jagged, like the pieces of the jigsaw puzzle in her head.

Length of body four feet, four inches, that was the height she had measured in the school that rainy afternoon, when she was all by herself in the classroom, the chairs and the desks empty. And that's the length of the body in the water, in a red dress, short sleeves. Bloating of features, peeling of epidermis, the water washes away the skin, she touches her face and in the water she sees the hands, the middle, ring and little fingers all have a gnawed effect. The face quivers with the water, its cheeks and chin dissolve, disappear. The words come back to her: bruising of the lips and tongue, brain and spinal cord liquefied. Her back hurts, she wants to get up but Alam says keep looking, there may be something that you missed the first time.

She keeps looking, the body turns in the water to show her multiple abrasions of various sizes, the heart softened and flabby, the blood rushes to her head, water swims in front of her eyes, her head spins. The skull is normal but the brain is liquefied.

Her hair falls across her face, she tucks it behind her ear, she can hear her breathing, her heart race. In the water the face has begun to change, eyes protruding. She closes her eyes and in the darkness smells the foetid, sick-sweet smell flowing past her. Drops splash on her face, on her clothes. Thoracic walls and ribs normal. She breathes in the morning air, lets it fill every pore in her body, fresh and cold.

Be careful, says Alam, don't worry, I'm standing here, and she bends down on her knees to touch the water and the face.

Bruising of the vaginal walls. The water flows faster, wets her clothes, pushes her backwards, grabs at her neck, like the shadow in her room that afternoon twenty years ago, says gently, don't worry, I won't hurt you, she is at home, drying herself, her clothes in a pile, the towel in her hands, bruising of the vaginal walls, each word slaps her in the face, on her breasts, her legs, in between, spelling pain and fear in black and white, says read me, listen to me, look at me, don't forget, don't brush away, she closes her eyes, the end of the towel is in her mouth now, another line from the report comes back to her, a gag is present, a folded handkerchief which is checked in colour, gag is completely blocking the pharynx, no, it wasn't checked in colour, it was white, she remembers, it was plain white. And, thank God, it didn't completely block the pharynx because she held it between her teeth, because she bit hard.

The face is gone, the water flows.

Mala can see the sunrise over the canal, lighting the water, green and black, with red and white.

Alam is still by her side. Behind them the water has receded so that there is a clearing between the houses again, waiting for her to walk, to take the left turn onto the street that will lead her to the market, back to her room in the hotel where she can pick up her bag, walk to the tea stall, wait for the bus and go home.

She wants to go home.

Mala returns

YOU CAN'T GO HOME like this, says Alam, standing behind her, crowding the tiny bathroom where Mala stands looking into the mirror; and he's right. The mud is everywhere: in her fingers, in her toes. The water has wrinkled the skin of both hands and feet. There's dirt under her clothes on her skin, she can feel its itch, its jabs. On her legs, on her back, the nape of her neck, behind her ears, above her breasts.

Give me your clothes, says Alam, they need to be washed. He waits in the bathroom.

From where she stands, in the centre of the room, flooded with sunlight, she can see a patch of the road outside through the window, so she walks to the corner of the room, at the foot of the bed, presses herself against the wall just in case someone is watching, just in case someone is flying outside, will land on the sill, take a peek. She plans to leave in a couple of hours, how will her clothes dry?

She lets the questions slip, like her clothes, into a pile on the floor.

Alam walks into the room, not looking, his eyes fixed below as he picks up her clothes, her jeans, her underwear, her shirt. On the way to the bathroom, he stops again, picks up the clothes she wore yesterday as well.

Let me do all of them, he says, why waste time.

She lies down on the bed, pulls the covers over her, the hotel has changed the bedsheet so it's fresh. She can hear the scrubbing, the soft soap against the hard clothes, the splash of water as Alam pours it out from a mug to wash the first layer of grime from the surface so that the soap can reach deep inside, into the pores of the fabric.

Quietly, she gets up, wraps the bedsheet around her, stands at the bathroom door to watch, the ends of the sheet trailing on the floor. His back is turned away from her, he is doing the collar of her shirt, using his nails to prise the dirt out. She sees the black water from the clothes flow into the drain, the white soap bubbles sliding between his fingers.

She keeps watching him wash her clothes, rinse, wash them again, wait for the water to drip. Then he drapes them, one by one, on the window sill, the smaller clothes on the window, the heavier ones on the chair.

And together, they wait for the wind.

She recalls how long ago, travelling in a train, she had dropped her handkerchief to the floor where it got soaked in a pool of water that someone had spilled. Her father was angry, her mother tied the handkerchief to the window, and she sat there, her face pressed to the iron bars, looking at the trees rush by, the tracks a blur, the handkerchief flapping hard as if it wanted to tug the train off the rails. By the next station, it was as dry as the air.

The wind begins to blow. She walks back to the bed and lies down, the sheet still draped over her.

*

Alam brings the towel, dipped in water that feels both warm and cold as he begins by wiping her feet, holding the edge of the towel so that it doesn't touch the bedsheet. He cleans each toe, the spaces in between, up the calves, rubs the dirt off her knees, wipes beneath them, in the hollows.

His fingers seek every turn in her body, every bend, moving up to her breasts, her armpits, she turns on her side, his hands move over her back, its ridges, over the mole near her waist, she shivers, he sees the gooseflesh, the crop of tiny dots on her skin, waits for it to settle down, then cleans her neck. With one hand, he gently pushes the hair away as he wipes the nape, the skin behind her ears, inside her ears, the tiny folds and the crevices, her chin, her lips, above the upper lip below her nose, her cheeks, the eyebrows, feels her eyelashes move against his palms. After the forehead, he moves down her shoulders, back to her arms, around the tiny wrinkle of skin near her elbows, the wrist, above and behind, her palm, its lines, her fingers and the nails.

She knows that she is naked now, the bedsheet is off her, she keeps her eyes closed. She can hear, over the sound of the towel against her body and the gentle noise of Alam's breathing – so gentle that she almost doesn't hear it as if he's holding his breath lest it wake her up – the wind rock the chair in the centre of the room. She can hear it make her clothes flap like kites in the sky, tied to her window by threads she cannot see.

When she opens her eyes, the wind has gone, taking Alam away with it along with her fear and her questions, leaving the clothes in her room dry, the ones she will wear spread out on the bed, the others neatly folded. And her body, clean. Outside, the sun has begun to set.

Mala waits for the bus at the tea stall.

Didi, you got your work done? the owner asks.

The boy's washing the glasses, she can hear the hiss of the gas.

Yes, she says.

What happened to that girl? Did you find out?

Nothing, she says.

See, I told you, I didn't hear anything about any girl being killed, he says, getting back to mixing the water and the milk.

The bus pulls over. Mala climbs on board, walks to an empty seat by the window. She looks out, she can see the small town slip away, house by house, tree by tree. The first to pass her by is the tea stall, she can see the boy get smaller. Then, the canal which now seems to be full of clean, blue water with trees lining its sides, the falling sunlight streaming through the branches, she can see flowers as well, a patch of colour, maybe that's a boat they have brought out for children to paddle in. She lowers her head, rests her chin on her wrist on the window frame, she can smell her arm, the soap and her shirt's washed fabric, she can see her nails glisten. She has never felt so clean before.

The conductor asks her for the fare, and as she takes out the change from her bag to pay him, the sheet of paper which is the post-mortem report, folded and creased in several places, falls out. The conductor doesn't notice as he hands her the ticket and goes back to stand near the door, on the footboard, to call out to the next lot of passengers. Mala bends down to pick up the sheet of paper, and midway, she changes her mind, she lets it be. The paper flaps once, twice, in the wind that enters the bus through the door and blows the paper underneath the seat in front.

She turns her face back to the window as the bus begins to fill up with strangers. First, in ones and twos, then in a steady trickle, bus stop by bus stop, until it becomes a flood, thick and heavy. She can feel the crowd lap against her, in front, to her left and right, the hotness of their breaths and the mixed smells of their talcum powder and sweat, the brush of someone's knees against hers as the bus lurches forward, swerves to avoid a ditch on the street.

Mala moves in her seat, draws her legs away from the crowd, pulls herself closer to one side as if she were trying to shrink herself so that she can escape through the window into the evening that's begun to seep blue black into the sky. She wants the bus to speed up, for the town to pass her rapidly by, for the city soon to appear, for the bus to stop in front of a building that from the street outside looks like a crying face and which is her home where her daughter lies, fast asleep. She wants to wake her up for dinner.

END OF PART TWO

THE THIRD PROLOGUE

'Wake up,' says Mother, 'you shouldn't go to sleep hungry.' The child lies on the bed, on her stomach, her face down, pressed so hard to one corner of the pillow that the other end is raised, like a gloved hand, white and upturned, across which is draped her black hair.

'Come, let's have dinner,' Mother puts four fingers of one hand on the child's bare shoulder, puts pressure, the child still doesn't move.

'Why were you standing on the balcony today, all alone?' Mother asks, going down on her knees on the floor until her face is almost level with the child's, her voice slightly louder than a whisper.

She can hear Father cough in the bedroom, she doesn't want him to hear.

'Father will be angry if you don't eat,' Mother says. 'He may beat both of us.'

The child moves, just a little bit, an inch or so.

I can make that out because I know how to see in the dark. Mother can't so she gets up, walks back to the dining table to clear up.

Five minutes later, she's back, the child lies still.

'I'm not eating dinner either,' Mother says, 'if you don't.'

Still no reply.

I'm standing on the window ledge, to the right of the balcony, leaning against the wall. I had to let the tired crow turn in for the night, the bird has flown across the city and the small town, braved the night and the day, the heat and the rain.

Mother walks onto the balcony, its edges are wet, glistening although the rain is now little more than a drizzle. There's a puddle of rain on the floor which she can't see in the dark. She steps into it, the ends of her sari stain black with water.

She stands there looking out as if the darkness will throw light on why her daughter was crying, why she's gone to bed hungry. But there's nothing here except for the black night, the black street and a dog. Brown. She can make out two white patches on its neck where something must have chewed at its fur, its tail little more than a stump.

It howls, barks a short bark, howls again.

She returns to the room and tries one more time.

'So I'm switching all the lights off,' she says, hoping this will make the child get up, scared.

The child doesn't move.

'Go to sleep,' Father calls out to Mother, 'leave her alone, you are the one who's spoiled her.'

Mother hears him but acts as if she hasn't. She can't get the crying out of her head.

The child is on her back now, her right hand over her eyes trying to block light which is not there, the street lights are off. The rain must have short-circuited some wire at the local substation. Mother can see what looks like a wet patch on the pillow, must be her tears.

She quietly closes the door that leads to the balcony, keeping it slightly ajar, a foot or so, to let the wind come in, keep the room fresh the entire night.

That's enough for me to squeeze in, to crawl across the floor, slip underneath the child's bed. And wait, quietly, for her to wake up, maybe for a glass of water.

I shall then tug at the end of her red dress, gently, so she doesn't get frightened. The child and I need to work together, I shall let her do the talking, I shall let her end this story. And I can help her if she listens to what I say, if she sees what I show. But then that's a very big if – as big and dark as the sky outside.

PART THREE

if

Once upon a time in my neighbourhood

ONCE UPON A TIME in my neighbourhood in the city, when I was between eleven and twelve years of age, late one night as I was fast asleep, through a little gap in the door that links my bedroom to the balcony outside, slipped in my friend, a strange-looking man, with a bunch of pictures in one pocket and, in the other, scraps of paper covered with his handwriting. He hid underneath my bed without making any noise, waited for one, two, two and a half hours – exactly how long he never said – but when I woke up in the middle of the night for a glass of water, he tugged at the end of my red dress. And almost made me trip.

No, this doesn't seem right, this isn't the way the story should begin, because long before my friend tugged at my red dress, before he hid underneath my bed, before he entered my room and even before I went to sleep, a strange little thing was happening in my neighbourhood: people, some young, some old, were killing themselves one by one, until at the end of a week or so, there were eight or ten deaths. More or less.

For the city, this isn't unusual since, on average, according to the Local Crime Records Bureau, almost three hundred and fifty people, plus or minus thirty, kill themselves every year; but because all these deaths happened in just one neighbourhood, newspapers began writing *Suicide Epidemic Hits City* and *Death Stalks City Neighbourhood*. Newspapers are like that.

The first to die was a girl who went to the same school as me, one class senior, she was very, very beautiful, had hair reaching down to her waist, hair that was untied when she slit her wrist with her father's blade, and they found her lying on the bed, her blood mixed with some shaving foam from the razor's edge.

No one knows why she did it, she didn't leave any note behind. Chandra, the maid, said that maybe no one liked her in school, which was hard to believe since during lunch she was always surrounded by girls who must have envied her, so beautiful she was. Mother says, maybe she was sad, for some reason.

Then it was Shah Uncle, the elder one of the two Shah brothers who run a telephone booth and a pastry shop at the end of the road. Father said he had taken a loan from a bank which he could not repay so he took his wife's shawl from the steel trunk which had only winter clothes, tied its corner around his neck and hanged himself from a hook on the ceiling.

The mothballs the shawl was wrapped in lay strewn across the floor when they came to pick up his body. But before they took him away to the crematorium, they brought his body to the shop, on a cot, with flowers and incense sticks, so that all could pay their last respects. Father went there as well. He said that Shah Uncle's eyes were open until his brother closed them and put a one-rupee coin on each to keep them that way.

And just before I came home from school that day, Mother says, she saw his wife crying, she couldn't even walk. Two women police constables had to hold her, one each side, and almost had to drag her back into her house.

That same night, when my parents had gone to sleep, and I was lying in my room, wide awake, the lights switched off, I thought of all kinds of things. Like what Shah Auntie was doing right now, was she sitting in a chair crying, was she sleeping, what would she do in the morning, would she make two cups of tea even though there was only one person in the house now. And it was then that I heard the noise.

I thought it was a cat jumping from one asbestos roof to the other. They all do that at night. Or the lid of some pot in some kitchen falling off, sliding on its own. But the noise never returned, and sometime later I fell asleep.

When I woke up the next morning, while I was preparing for school, arranging my exercise books, brushing my hair, Chandra told us about Bomba, the boy downstairs. He had left a note for his parents, saying he was killing himself because he had been a bad boy and would now never bother them. But the rope he used couldn't take his weight and snapped, making him fall down to the floor, hurt himself. They took him to the hospital and put his leg in a cast. Chandra said Bomba's maid told her the story.

After the first few incidents, people began talking in whispers, outside Mr Das's sweet shop where they stood in line while he weighed the curd and the sweets; at the butcher's down the street while they waited for him to skin the meat, wash the blood away. At the bus stop right in front of the post office, sometimes inside the post office, too. And when you walked by, especially if you were not a grown-up, these people would stop talking, afraid you might listen. For, Mother says, young people are the ones most likely to kill themselves.

She was wrong because then the old cobbler died.

I knew him very well since Father got him to polish his shoes. He also used to stitch my school bag whenever its buckle snapped. Just like new, he would always say when he handed the shoes or the bag back to us. He was about seventy, eighty years old, very poor, he used to spread a piece of cloth on the pavement beside the lamp post, use four stones to hold its four corners down, and then set up his stall there.

His eyes were so weak, his glasses so strong that one day when he had kept them by his side and was taking a nap, leaning against the cement slab which was the base of the lamp post, the sunlight got focused so sharp through his lenses that a piece of paper in which he had wrapped a bunch of iron nails caught fire. And had it not been for the smoke waking him up, making him cough, everything he owned in this world would have burned down.

One morning, Chandra again – she was always the one with the news – came running to our house and said that the cobbler had walked into the path of a bus which was on its way to the airport and had been run over. Some people think this was an accident, she said, but no, I don't think so. Because he knew this street inside out, I had seen him cross it several times every day and there's no way he could have made such a mistake.

After the cobbler, came the others – strangers with neither names nor faces. Two men, a woman and a child, and I heard about their deaths in scraps of conversation that floated across the neighbourhood and sometimes furtively entered our house. Like the story of the mechanic who hanged himself above a lathe in the metal-cutting shop because he had lost his job. He had made a copy of the keys, and at night, had entered the shop, switched all the machines on and then hanged himself from the ceiling, his feet inches away from the lathe's bed. Or the one about the bus conductor who drank Baygon Spray after his child died of malaria. Or the woman who jumped off the terrace because her husband would beat her every night.

Whether these were the actual reasons behind these deaths, I can never tell. But that didn't stop people from saying all sorts of things. In fact, at school, Miss would bring newspaper clippings and pin them on the board, ask us to read them carefully and write summaries of their reports which dealt with ways and means to prevent the deaths.

One said, after the first girl's death, that razor blades should be taken away from all homes and all fathers be asked to get themselves shaved at the two barber shops in the neighbourhood. That all knives be removed and arrangements made for the local market to sell vegetables, already cut and peeled.

Another said that all hooks on all ceilings should go since these were the ones most often used by people to hang themselves. And instead of ceiling fans, all homes should be asked to use stand-fans, their blades locked in a cage with wire mesh so thin that no one can slip a finger inside, get hurt.

A third newspaper called for schools to take urgent steps: hold classes only on the ground floor and that, too, only in those rooms where windows are low so that if a child wants to jump off, all she can do is to break a few bones, not take her life.

And to make slitting of the wrists more difficult, someone said seize all sharp-edged instruments from geometry boxes, dividers and compasses, ban all pens so that nibs can't be used, even pencil sharpeners, the kind where you can unscrew the top and take the blade out.

I asked Mother about the deaths and she said people kill themselves when they are very sad, when they live in very sad houses and have nowhere to go. Which made me worried because if you stand at the bus stop and look at our house, it looks like a crying face. Its windows are the eyes, half-closed by curtains, while the rain, wind and sun have marked the wall, streaked several lines, two of which look like tears, one below each window. The mouth is the balcony, curved down under the weight of iron railings, rusted and misshapen. Like the stained teeth of someone sad, someone very old.

So this is how things are in the neighbourhood when late one night, when everyone has gone to sleep, my friend slips into my room, hides beneath my bed, without making any noise, and when I wake up in the middle of the night for a glass of water, he tugs at the end of my red dress. And although I'm only between eleven and twelve years of age, I'm not afraid one bit. Maybe it's because of the way he tugs at my dress. Like a friend, gently.

My friend

AT FIRST, I almost trip, I think I have caught the dress in my toe. Or in a nail that must have come unstuck in the wooden frame of the bed, but when he tugs a second time, I look down and there he is, crawling out from underneath the bed, cobwebs and dust balls in his hair. Still crouching on the floor, he begins to move towards the balcony, and when he reaches the centre of the room, he stops, suddenly. The moonlight enters through the gap in the door and falls on his face as he turns to me and says, I am your friend.

Why did you sneak in? I ask.

I had to, he says, there was no other way.

What do you mean you are my friend? I haven't ever seen you, I say.

No, he says, you did see me, in the evening. I saw you, too.

You must be lying, I say, tell me one reason why I should talk to you.

I could have tripped you up, he says, you could have fallen on your face, hurt yourself, I didn't do that.

This doesn't sound convincing and he can see that on my face.

Well, listen carefully, he says, I am going to tell you

something but I am going to tell it very fast and I am not going to repeat it.

And then he takes a long breath, closes his eyes and begins speaking, without moving the slightest inch, without pausing even once, not even for a breath. In a whisper so loud and so clear that I'm afraid my parents may wake up.

This is what he says:

You were standing on the balcony crying this evening when Father was in the room behind you taking his shoes off he then got up to wash his hands and his face and Mother served him dinner but he wanted some more salt he always asks for extra salt and she went to the kitchen to get some and when his dinner was over and Mother took his dishes back to the kitchen you walked back to your room and went to sleep crying and hungry and although Mother tried to wake you up you didn't and I know why you were crying you were crying because of the people dying in the neighbourhood and this has made you afraid that your father or your mother may kill themselves or maybe even you since sometimes standing on the balcony and looking down you have often thought how would it be if you let go what would happen if you fell down to the street below.

I can hear his breath as he lets go.

Who are you? I ask.

I told you I am your friend, he says, as he walks across the room and opens the door, his steps so confident and measured as if this were his house and I the one who has sneaked in. He walks onto the balcony, sits on his haunches, leans his back against the wall, balances himself on his heels and his toes so that his feet don't get wet in the puddle on the floor left by the rain.

I have come here to help you, he says.

Help me, with what? I ask. And speak softly, I don't want anyone to wake up.

I have come here to tell you that you don't need to be afraid of the suicides any more.

What about my parents? I ask. Are they going to kill themselves?

No, they won't, says my friend, and I will make sure that you won't, either.

How can you be so sure? I ask.

And he says: I know, that's why I've been sent here. I was told that while people were killing themselves in your neighbourhood, your parents never once thought of doing the same. I came here to find out why. Because I figured that if I can come up with an answer that explains their living, maybe I can stop others from dying.

All this sounds very heavy, very complicated but my friend says, I will explain, I have got pictures to show you, I have got stories to tell. And therein lies the answer. I need your help to understand.

He takes out an envelope from his shirt pocket, pats and smooths its edges out. There are pictures in here, he says, pictures of your Father as I followed him the whole day today. And then I wrote down what I saw when I followed your Mother today.

And neither of them noticed a thing? I ask.

No, not a thing, he says.

How come? I ask.

Because, you see, he says, I am the Champion of Hide and Seek.

The Champion of Hide and Seek

I CAN SEE WHY he calls himself this – why, if he hides, he will remain hidden; and why, if he seeks, he can seek anything out. That's the way he is, take a careful look at him and you will understand. His face is dark, which means in twilight he can slip into the purple shade; at night, he can melt into the black shadows. His skin is deep brown so during the day he can hide behind wooden doors, and if he wears a light green shirt with leafy prints, he can even climb up a tree and the birds won't notice.

His feet are large, slightly curved below the instep, which helps him balance himself on window sills and terrace ledges, with no fears of tumbling down while he listens in on a conversation inside to which he's not invited. The soles of his shoes have clasps that help him get a firm grip, if he takes them off, his socks are made of a special kind of towel fabric, the kind of cloth which has thick, tiny threads sticking out, cut and curled, that mesh with the jagged surface of a fence. Or the rough plaster on a wall.

He has extra muscles in his eyes which make him squint sharper, quicker when he looks through keyholes. His palms are cupped on their own so that he needs little effort to look through frosted glass, through cracks in walls, between gaps in doors. Or through a window in a dark room into the night.

His lungs are large, he can hold his breath so that if he's hiding behind curtains they never move to give him away.

His ears are special as well. From the outside, you can't see anything unusual, but take one of those torches that doctors use, the ones that come with special lenses, switch off all the lights in the room, and look. You will find that the membrane, the one that's stretched tightly inside, which vibrates with any sound that falls on it, is in his case much thinner, more sheer, more transparent, you can see the blood flowing, the balancers moving, everything. That's why he can hear the slightest of sounds, he can hear what people say under their breaths; looking at their lips, he can make out their words, even when they sleep and mumble in their dreams.

That's why when he followed Father and Mother today, he says, neither of them noticed anything even as he took pictures, took notes, while he watched and listened, saw and felt.

Now I need your help to understand, are you ready?

His eyes have begun to sparkle, his clothes are soaked, which is strange since it's not raining now, it must be his sweat. His shoes look worn, I can see his instep, curved; his cupped palms smudged as if he's been playing with children in the mud or looking through dirty window-panes. His hair's streaked with cobwebs, he must have hidden in some corner that's not been cleaned for quite some time.

Are you ready? he asks again.

Yes, I say, and he brings out, from his pocket, a large envelope.

Hold on, let me check once, I say.

And just to be doubly sure that my parents are asleep, I run into the house, stand near the door to their bedroom. I can see the rise and the fall of Mother's chest, Father lies on his stomach, one hand draped over the side of the bed. Both are asleep, the road is clear.

Everything is safe, I tell him, let us begin.

And he says, first I have to give you a little bit of background.

A little bit of background

FOLLOWING YOUR Father was easy, he says, much easier than I had expected. Because for most of the time, we were outside, on the street, never once did I have to stop suddenly, slip into a shop or a narrow lane, press myself flat against a wall, hide behind somebody else. Or even hold my breath. I kept walking, several paces behind him, and maybe it was the rain that helped because he kept stopping for shelter which gave me some time to rest as well, to catch my breath.

Taking his pictures wasn't difficult either. At first, I was worried Father would hear the camera's click, but once we were outside, the sounds of the city, ebbing and rising, filled the gaps of silence in between. So much so that I could have called out his name and he wouldn't have heard. For what's the click of a camera amid the noise of a bus or a truck revving its engine, cars and taxis on wet roads, splashing water, shopkeepers calling out to customers to stop, customers shouting to bring down the price? And over and above this, the heavy raindrops falling, all at once, on umbrellas, on the roofs of houses, the asbestos sheets on the buses. A click? I wasn't worried at all.

Not that I was always confident, no, there were times

I was nervous my cover would be blown, there were moments I could hear my heart race. Like when I tripped once, stumbled across a manhole cover they had removed and put back but not quite right so that a bit of it jutted out of the ground, and found myself barely inches away from Father, so close I could almost count the raindrops in his hair.

At another time, in the tram when Father was on his way back home, the driver suddenly applied the brakes, making me lurch forward, and because I wasn't holding on to anything, the camera in my hand, I bumped into him, he was sitting looking out of the window.

He turned, our eyes met but he turned away again.

The most difficult part, however, was when I was in Father's office. There I was tried and tested, I had to use all the skills I have, even had to come up with new ones, then and there.

There were times when every muscle in my body was stretched, strained, every nerve ached when I had to hide behind doors. Once, I had to slip in with the sweeper, crouch behind his bucket, move behind his broom, suck in my breath so hard I became as thin as I could. Then I had to bribe a little boy who carries tea into the office so that I could take the tray from him, go in, the camera hidden between my palm and the glasses.

That's why some pictures became blurred, distorted. As if they were taken by two lenses at the same time.

Where are the pictures, I ask, can I look?

Wait, he says, don't be impatient, let me first tell you about Mother, because that's a different story altogether.

Following Mother was, in a way, the opposite of following Father because she never left home except for a brief while at the end when she went to the tea stall to wait for your school bus. Which meant that I had to be, for all practical purposes, in two places at the same time, with Father and with Mother, outside on the street, inside at home.

So I would follow Father for a while, wait until he settled down in some place for an hour or so, then rush back home to watch Mother, wait for her to lie down on the bed, fall asleep for a while, and then run back to Father.

Had it not been for the rain, people would have noticed me. Who is this strange man who keeps running to the bus stop, returning again, running to the house, running out, taking a bus again. By the end of the day, I had travelled so far – by bus, by tram, sometimes by taxi, often on foot – that I don't think I will be able to walk for a long time to come.

Getting back to Mother, it was very very difficult.

Father was easy, he was in the open, in the crowd, he walked and he stopped, he walked and he stopped, giving me time to watch and wait. But Mother stayed at home the entire day, she kept moving from one room to the other, and even when she sat down, it was for such a short time that I was constantly on the move, trying my best to remain hidden, to remain unseen and unheard. So when she went to the kitchen, I slithered across the living room floor, crawled between the chairs and then peeped into the kitchen. When she came back to the living room, I hid underneath the bed, saw her feet pace up and down, lift the chairs, put them back again, arrange the pillows, the bedsheet; and when she went to the bedroom, where she spent the most time, I climbed up the wall and hid between the rafters in the ceiling. Being inside the house meant I couldn't take any pictures. I couldn't use the camera since everything was quiet, the click or the flash would have given me away, so I took pictures in the mind and later I wrote down what I saw.

I have sifted through everything, chosen the best Father pictures, the ones that came out clear, four of them in the order in which they were taken. Look at the pictures and describe each one to me, see what you can add, and if words fail you, if you fall short, don't worry, I shall fill in the blanks.

As for Mother, I have written down what I saw, what I heard, I have made it short and simple so that you can understand. Read it, tell me if you have any questions.

And he hands me the pictures and the scraps of paper, one by one.

It's my turn to speak, he is quiet, leaning against the balcony wall, he closes his eyes and listens.

Picture, text, picture, text

THE FIRST PICTURE is postcard size, five inches by six inches, like the ones I see in the window of 'Flash Express', the studio near Park Street where Father took us one day for a group photo. My friend took this picture in the morning when it was raining very, very heavily but you can't make that out. That's because my friend's camera is a very old model, he can't adjust the time or the speed, also you need a special film, he says, which he doesn't have, so in the first picture, all I can see of the rain are puddles on the street. No one's walking on the street in the picture except one man, maybe it's a woman, you can't tell, wrapped in plastic. The face is blurred, the ankles are bare, so are the feet.

I know this street, it's the one Mother and I take when we go to the market in the evening and the pavement is too crowded to walk on. My favourite shop – it's not here in the picture but it's just a couple of metres away from where the picture ends – sells dolls, all dressed up, with golden, curled hair, their faces the colour of sunset, their eyes that of the sky. The one I like most has a red dress with flowers on the front, white and blue, its sleeves have frills made of lace. Father says we don't have the money yet, I need to wait.

Some days, on this same street, there's a man with a crow and there's a crowd all around. He promises to fly people on the back of his crow, across and beyond the city. Mother thinks he's just a conman, Father says no, it could be real, you never know.

There's a dog in this picture, too, brown in colour, but just a bit of it. It must have been in the frame, but just when my friend clicked, it must have run away because you can see only its tail. It's cut at one end, something has chewed at its fur.

On the left, at the very edge of the frame, is Father.

He's in his black trousers and his white shirt, that's his office dress, he has two pairs of black trousers. He says that just as I have a school uniform, ash-coloured skirt and a white shirt, he has one for his office as well.

Father's standing underneath a shelter right across the street from the bus stop. He has the newspaper over his head, like a cap. He's waiting for the rain to slow down so that he can step out, run to the bus stop, without drenching his clothes.

He's standing at the Shimla Post Office. Its entrance has no awning, no shelter, it's flush with the pavement, not even a single step above or below. This is his favourite place, he always stands here even if it's not raining, every day. And it's only when he can see the bus coming that he crosses the street.

In the picture, Father's looking inside. He must be looking at the man who sits in a corner right near the entrance and writes letters for those who can neither read nor write. He's about Father's age, he even looks a little like Father, and like him he wears black trousers. On his desk, he keeps all sorts of things, inlands, envelopes, postcards, a bottle of glue and a piece of cotton wool. He also has a candle, a matchbox, a stick of wax, a needle and a thread.

Whenever Father and I go to the post office to buy stamps, send letters, he keeps looking at this man. Some days he goes there and listens to the letters that he writes and then tells us about them at dinner.

One day he told me about a boy who was sending money home for his sister.

Chandra goes to this man whenever she has to send money home. One day the man wasn't there and Chandra got her letter written by Father. Father was very happy, he says he likes doing this, writing letters for other people. Sometimes he says that if he were lucky, if he had been alone, he would have done this. But now he has Mother and I to take care of.

*　　*　　*

My friend brings out the first sheet of paper and I read:

After you leave for school, for Mother there are a thousand and one things to do. Chandra has already done the dishes, swept and scrubbed the floors, made the bed, fluffed the pillows, aired the bedsheets, but when Mother moves from one room to the other, her eyes pick up the pillows, not in a straight line. One pillowcase hasn't been pulled all the way down so she picks it up, pats it back into shape, fluffs it again, places it on the bed, moves a few steps back to see if she's got it right. No, it's now at an angle to the other, a couple of inches off to the right, she pushes it to the left, now they are in one straight line but the movement of the pillows has rumpled the bedsheet, two creases run diagonally, she tugs at the end that overhangs the bed until the creases are gone.

Now the bed is perfect.

Almost.

The bed out of her mind and her way, at least for now, she looks at the floor. It's clean, she can see the marks the scrubbing has left but what she's drawn to are the specks around the chair's legs. She goes to the kitchen to get the mop, it's behind the gas cylinder, she wets it in the sink, the tap is dry so she has to take water from the bucket in a glass and pour it onto the mop. She watches the water stain the cloth, wrings it just a little bit, she doesn't want the water to drip as she goes from the sink to the room but she wants the wetness to stay so she cups the mop in her hands. And bends down to wipe the rings from the chair legs away.

Now that she has the mop in her hand, what else should be done?

The showcase.

She cleaned it the day before yesterday, it's shut tight, the dust wouldn't have entered through the glass door but why take a chance? The first shelf has a brass Buddha, two ashtrays made of stained glass, the second has three dolls. She stands there for a while, perhaps thinks about the doll you want, the one in the shop, in the red dress.

When we buy it, I will put it here, with the three other dolls, she decides.

She looks at the other shelves, they are crowded,

there's a stuffed kangaroo, a box of marbles, an incense stick holder made of sandalwood, shaped like a candle with a wide base for the ash to fall and collect.

She lifts one ashtray, one more thin spread of dust, she wipes it with a cloth, does the same for the Buddha and the dolls. She will do the rest later, she closes the door, checks to see whether her fingers have left a smudge, none that she can see but she wipes it again anyway.

On her way back to the kitchen with the mop, she passes the balcony.

It's raining.

She closes the door although the rain is very light, and goes into the kitchen. The shelves have to be cleaned.

She climbs onto a chair and removes the jars one by one. The jar with the rice is the biggest one, it's made of glass with a cap that's coloured blue in which she sees her face, distorted, her forehead merging with her chin, both elongated, her eyes slits, the ends of her sari slip revealing her blouse. It doesn't matter, no one's looking. She brings the jar down, puts it on the kitchen counter, adjusts her sari and gets onto the chair again.

All the jars are on the counter now. The newspaper she had spread on the shelf to protect the wood has turned yellow, stained with oil and lines of spices that have fallen from the jars and scattered, turmeric, cinnamon, cloves, yellow, green and brown. This needs to be changed so she folds the newspaper, crumples it, drops the roll behind the door, near the gas cylinder, the maid will take it with the garbage tomorrow.

She needs a fresh newspaper to put on the shelf. Yesterday's paper, that's what Father always leaves for her,

*says no harm if you read the newspaper one day late. She
fetches it from the living room and spreads it on the shelf,
fold by fold. She needs all the sixteen pages.*

*She has to move the chair to the left and the right to
spread the paper out evenly. As she smoothes the folds,
tucks the paper in the corners, around the edges, she
reads the headlines* – Governor Lays Foundation Stone
for School, Girl Found Dead in Small Town, Transport
Strike Likely Today.

*Still standing on the chair, she reads about a girl, eleven
or twelve years of age, who was found dead in a small
town. It's just two paragraphs, something about what
was written in a post-mortem report, about a girl, roughly
your age, who was found strangled in a canal flooded with
rain.*

*   *   *

The second picture is of Father in his office. Father has
told us that at work he has a room of his own. That it
has a green carpet on the floor. That he has an assistant
to get him his tea, pick up the phone when he's out on his
inspection tours. He's told us that, as a very important
officer in the City Building Clearance Office, he has a
large mahogany desk with a velvet cover, an ante-room
where visitors come and wait with their building plans.
And a generator which runs twenty-four hours a day even
on Sundays. On some evenings when he comes home to a
power cut, he lights the lantern so that Mother can cook
dinner and I can do my homework, and says that if the
power doesn't come until late in the night, he will go to

the office and sleep on the sofa because there, the power is always on.

But the picture shows nothing of this.

It's the picture of a room with bare walls, there are dirty marks on the wall where the plaster has chipped in several places. Father's sitting at a desk, the surface of which is wood, chipped, there's a paperweight on the desk, there's no telephone. His chair is a swivel chair with blue upholstery, made of something that looks in the picture like velvet. It's torn, both in the backrest and the armrest, with stuffing coming out.

He's looking at his desk, his head lowered, a pen in his hand, its cap on. But there's no paper, I think he's just looking at either the pen or the surface of the desk. Behind him is a window with a pane missing. The lower half is boarded with newspapers and Scotch tape. It's difficult to read what's written on the newspapers because Father is blocking the view.

I don't know what Father does, which makes it difficult for me at school since most of my friends say that their fathers have taken them to their offices, shown them around. Once I asked Father what he did and he said you won't understand, it's very complicated.

Mother, I think, knows what Father does.

She told me one day that he sits in the office, collects plans of buildings, keeps them in a file, ready for the engineers. Every one who wants to construct a building in this city has to get a map done first, and only when Father's office stamps it, says it is safe, it won't fall down, that it has been designed as per the rules, can they start building.

Sometimes, when we receive gifts at home, Father says

those are from people whose buildings his office has approved. That was how we got the gas stove. Mother got angry, said the old one was working all right and it was wrong to get something we didn't pay for, but Father said, we don't have the money to buy a new one, so accept it, it will help you, it has burners with an electronic lighter built in so she won't have to search for matches any more.

He has told her that soon they are going to build a very special building in the city, called Paradise Park, it's going to be the tallest building in the city and he will have to look at its plan; and when it's approved, we will get several gifts, a washing machine and a new television set and maybe, if I'm lucky, the doll in the red dress as well, the dress with little flowers on the front, white and blue.

* * *

The newspaper stares at her as if it wants to be read. Mother begins putting the jars back, one by one, the ones she uses most often in the front, the others in the back, against the wall. But the newspaper keeps staring at her so she stops again, goes back to read the item about the girl found dead in the small town, looks at an advertisement showing a woman in blue jeans and a white shirt, with a leather bag slung over her shoulder.

She steps down from the chair, her hands stained with dust, marked with the colour of spices. She washes them once again, then looks around the kitchen. There's a tiny window in the wall, a few feet above the gas stove. It seems she hasn't opened it in a long time because the window is jammed. She has to push extra hard and it opens with a sudden lurch. Through it, she can see the iron pipes that run right down the building. Two sparrows have made their nest there.

So many times have her hands come in contact with water that the skin on her fingers is wrinkled. She walks to the dressing table, looks in the mirror. She leans forward, stretches the skin below her eyes. She can see the faint sign of a double chin, she sucks hard, it disappears. She picks up the tube of cold cream lying on the dressing table, it's wrinkled, its ends turned up. She applies some to her hands, it will keep her skin soft.

Passing the window, she can see the rain. On the sill there is a wet crow, its wings all rumpled. It shakes itself hard, once, twice, then flies away. Maybe like you, she remembers the story of the man with the crow that Father talked about, the crow that can fly you across and beyond the city.

A raindrop has formed on the wooden frame. She brings her face closer to it, her eyes are now almost against the drop, which slowly, right in front of her eyes, begins to grow as the earth pulls its weight to the centre of its gravity. It's now a big drop, like a pearl, and just before it breaks away, she puts her finger to the bottom, very very gently.

She holds her breath, almost as if the drop were alive, a strange, spherical insect made of glass, all eyes and nothing else, shimmering and transparent, it will fly away if she isn't careful. Her finger touches, the drop breaks, cold and wet. She waits for the second to form. And she does the same again, she watches it grow, she touches it, watches it break.

* * *

It is evening in the third picture, the rain has stopped but the street is wet, the lights reflected in the puddles.

This is Park Street, my friend says.

I have been there, about three or four times, maybe five. Once Father took Mother and I before Durga Puja when we had to buy new clothes but he said don't buy anything in Park Street, it's very expensive, you will get the same things in the neighbourhood market at half the price.

My friend has taken the picture standing from the street, at one corner, so that there are a row of shops, all with lights on.

On the pavement, you can see the stalls that sell things made in China and Japan, a girl in my class bought a lipstick there, it's pink and very smooth, she let me use it once but just before going home I had to wash it off because Mother would get angry.

Father is looking into a shop window where they have stuck posters. Two of them are blurred in the picture, two are very clear. It's the bookshop called 'Readers' Heaven'. The poster Father is looking at shows two tall buildings with hundreds and hundreds of floors rising into the sky. The buildings, one on either side of the street, seem to be tilting towards one another as if they meet somewhere high above. There is a narrow strip of sky in between.

Look closely, my friend says, look at what's between the two buildings below. I bring the picture closer to my eyes and all I see is a patch of darkness that's the shadow from the buildings, but once my friend points out a car, I can see it.

It's a street and people are walking on either side on the pavement. Very tiny people, I can't see their faces, but they are wearing black coats, one of them is wearing a hat. There's also a tree on the street, surrounded by a fence made of wire, the leaves are black with white patches on some. This is a city in a foreign country, says my friend, the white patches are the snow.

The second poster is that of a woman, a very very beautiful woman, just her face, her hair black and straight, brushed back, falling to her shoulders in one smooth wave. She is fair, very fair, almost white. She looks like a filmstar, like the ones they have in Mitra Cinema where they show English films.

* * *

It's raining harder. Mother can hear the drops drum against the window, on the street. She makes a quick tour of the house again perhaps to double-check on the windows. All are closed, one is slightly broken, she has boarded it with plywood and a piece of paper.

She walks into the living room and from the cupboard she takes out a photo album. It's got a cover made of red velvet held in place by a gold spiral. She opens the album to its first page, there's a picture of a little girl, maybe her when she was a child, with her mother. She looks at it for a long time. Another one has the same girl, this time sitting on a man's lap; the next is the man, perhaps her father, your grandfather, sitting at a desk, in front of a typewriter, a newspaper by his side. She flips these pages, doesn't even stop to look, keeps flipping until she reaches the section where her wedding pictures begin.

Your father is there in one picture, all by himself, with a bridegroom's cap on, its white tassels draped over his face, smiling at the person who took the picture. There's one of her with many, many people, perhaps her relatives, old and young, men, women and children, boys and girls.

There's one picture of two cooks pouring buckets and buckets of rice into a huge aluminium tub, then stirring the vegetables with a bamboo pole. In one, fishes are stacked on one side on what looks like a terrace, their heads cut, the entire floor littered with their scales.

The picture which she keeps looking at for a long time, tilting the page of the album so that she can get a better look, is dark, it has been taken at night since the background is black. She's getting into a white car decked with flowers. There are bright lights in the picture, there is a wedding band, two men in white stand around a bright lamp and are playing trumpets. A boy holds a sparkler in his hand.

The room gets dark so she closes the album, walks to your study table, the one in the living room. She switches on the lamp, looks at your books, picks one out. She flips the pages.

* * *

This is the fourth and the last picture, taken inside a tram. My friend says this was the most difficult one to take since, even in the first class coach, the lights are very dim. So my friend had to use a flash, the question was when and how. Out on the street, it was easy; inside the tram, it was a whole different thing.

But he was lucky. Just when the tram entered the Maidan stretch, was about to take that sweeping arc before it reached its terminus, it stopped, everything went off, it was dark. Someone shouted accident, accident.

No, said the conductor, give us five minutes, we will set it right, please don't panic. What had happened was that the long iron arm on top of the tram which links it to the wires above and through which the tram gets its power had slipped out of its groove. The conductors, helped by the driver, got out of the tram, tugged at the thick cord that hangs from the arm and tried to slide it back into place. They couldn't get it right the first time but eventually it slid into place, power was restored, the lights came on, the engine began to hum, the tram shuddered. And then it slid again, everything was dark again.

Three times, my friend says, the arm slipped and three times it slid into place so that there were three flashes inside. And he took three pictures, no one even noticed.

Because there's a flash, the last picture is clear, all the light concentrated on Father who is sitting by the window, looking out into the dark.

He is looking at the Maidan. I can also see some lights outside the tram, those must be the blue and white ice-cream vendors who stand in front of the Victoria Memorial, many of them have lights on top of their vans. I have been there a few times on Sundays when the Maidan is crowded but so big is the Maidan that it never seems crowded, you always get a place to run around without bumping into anybody. Once Father bought me an ice cream there.

Father's looking out of the window, his chin in his hand, his elbow rests on the brown, wooden frame. So sharp is the picture that I can see a drop of water near his elbow, someone must have spilled it from a glass or a water bottle.

He's sitting right in front because, on the left of the picture, I can see the wire mesh wall which is the entrance to the driver's cabin, there's something written there too but in very small letters.

The newspaper that he used as a hat in the morning as he stood in the post office is now crumpled on his lap, sliding down. Father looks tired, there are stains on his shirtsleeves. His face I can't see in full but his shirt collar is pushed back so that the breeze can fan his neck.

Look above his head, my friend says, what do you see there?

There's a blur of blue and white as if someone has drawn something and then tried to erase it away.

No, look carefully, go back to the earlier picture, he says, the one on Park Street where Father is looking at the posters in the shop window. Look at the posters and then come back to this picture.

I do exactly as he says. At first, I don't notice anything and then it becomes clear, so clear that I'm surprised it didn't strike me the first time. Above Father's head, inside the tram, there is a poster, and on the poster, the face of a woman, she looks exactly the same as the woman in the bookstore, very very beautiful, white, her hair short reaching up to her shoulders, her eyes this time looking at Father.

* * *

Mother looks at her watch, it's time for you to come home from school so she picks up the umbrella, walks down the two flights of stairs, crosses the street and waits at the tea stall where your bus will drop you off.

She sits on the bench. In front of her, against the mud wall, is Mr Sarkar, the owner, sitting behind an oven, his face half hidden by the huge aluminium kettle, its sides as black as coal, licked by flames, blue and yellow.

Didi, how are you today? Sarkar asks, the kettle in his hand poised above the gas stove, there is no other customer at this time.

Have a cup of tea, he says, it's the first one this afternoon, I am using a fresh set of tea-leaves, the morning's stock is over.

Yes, she says.

She looks at the small earthen shelf carved into the wall, there are three plastic jars, all identical, one packed with biscuits, the other with chocolates, their shiny wrappers dulled through the jar's dirty plastic. He should clean it with soap and water. She buys two chocolates for you.

The rain drums on the tin roof of the stall, the water and the milk boil, the hiss of the gas is very loud. She looks at a little boy who washes the spoons and the glasses. His shirt is drenched with sweat and rain. She watches Sarkar use a brown towel as a filter, wring the tea out, open the towel to empty the leaves back into the kettle.

The rain gets heavier, water is now streaming down from the roof in tiny rivulets that splash on the ground, churn the mud. She looks at the empty street, a truck passes.

Come inside, you will get wet, Sarkar says.

The tea is ready, it's very hot, scalding, she blows into the glass, sees her breath mix with the steam, she keeps her face over the glass for a while.

What's this I hear about the suicides? Sarkar asks.

Mother's glass ready, he is taking a break, he's got up from his seat behind the stove and is now standing beside her, wiping the bench.

Yes, I hope all this ends soon, she says.

The rain keeps falling. She looks at the drops, she can hear the gas flame, your bus turns around the corner.

*   *   *

You can keep the pictures and the notes with you, my friend says. Look at them whenever you are afraid.

Why? I ask, I don't understand.

You will understand when it's all over, he says, there are some things still left.

What do we need to do now? I ask, it's getting colder, the night is blackest now, must be just a few hours away from dawn.

Let's listen to your father and mother in the dark when

they are in bed, both of them together. You want to join me? he asks.

Yes, I say.

But before we do that, one last thing, he says. When you were on the balcony, while your Father was taking his shoes off, his eyes were fixed on the page of a book lying on the table. It was the same book that Mother was looking at earlier in the afternoon when you had gone to school. Why don't you get me the book, it's still lying on the table. I want to know what they were looking at.

And still sitting on the balcony, he points at the book which I can see through the door. It's my school textbook, lying open on the cracked glass top of the table in the centre of the room.

My school textbook

THE BOOK he points to is my school textbook *Learning English*. The word *Learning* is in yellow, *English* is in blue, both words are printed in a type that doesn't look like type, it looks like handwriting, cursive, on a black rectangle on the cover. They have drawn the rectangle to make it look like a blackboard, it has a red frame running all around, and two straight lines angled towards each other: these are the strings tied to two tiny hooks from which the blackboard hangs on the wall.

The back cover is white with just one line at the bottom: *Printed at the Government Printing Press, Park Street.*

My father works at the City Building Clearance Office on Park Street.

I have spent so much time with this book, I tell my friend, that I know most of it by heart. With my eyes closed, I can tell you what it looks like. I can read out chapters line for line, word for word. Like the one called 'Robert Bruce', about the brave king who took shelter in a cave in a far-off land after his enemies drove him away from the kingdom.

Which is your favourite chapter? My friend asks. Is

there a chapter that your father and mother read with you, help you with when you do your homework?

That's Chapter Number Three, I say, it's called 'Describing People'.

Open the book to that chapter, he says.

I turn the pages, they turn without making any noise. We read by the moonlight.

This chapter has drawings of several characters and a paragraph below each.

My favourites are Rima, she is slim, she has an oval face, she has a sharp nose, hair that falls to her shoulders like a wave, she's wearing a blue sari. Her skin is white, like foreigners have. And Alam, he is a thin man, he wears a blue shirt and black trousers and has a belt with a big buckle.

Rima and Alam, says my friend, these are very uncommon names.

Now let's go inside, he says, let's go and listen to your parents as they lie in the dark.

Listening in the dark

WE CRAWL, my friend and I, we slither across the floor, we cross the living room, he in front, I behind him, holding his leg. We enter my parents' bedroom. By this time, so long have I stayed up in the dark that my eyes have adjusted, I can make out all the shapes, even the blades of the ceiling fan. Maybe its wire is loose, it makes a noise which is convenient since we need sound in this quiet hour to cover our own.

The window is closed. Father and Mother are lying on the bed, their backs turned to each other. That's a problem since on both sides of the bed – there are two pairs of eyes – we have to be extra careful as we slide under the bed. The ends of the bedspread scrape our backs but this sound is too soft to be heard.

It takes a minute for us to settle down, pull our legs and hands so that we are underneath the bed.

First, I need to slow down my heart which by now is racing so hard I can hear it. I have been holding my breath since I entered the room, I have never done this before, sneaked in on my parents like this. My chest, my lungs are full of air which I exhale very slowly. It hurts.

As luck would have it, we can hear the rain, it's started again, taps the window sill, knocks on the glass pane.

Together with the fan, the wind and the rain will, hopefully, muffle the sounds we make. We are safe, whispers my friend.

The underside of the bed is not as dirty as I'd thought, I can't feel any cobwebs, when I run my fingers against the floor, there's no dust, it's cold, clean. Mother scrubbed this after she picked you up from school, says my friend.

There's a creak, someone moves. I can hear their breaths now but these aren't breaths of sleep, regular and rhythmic, these are breaths of waking, shorter. I hear a cough, this is Mother.

'It's started to rain again,' she says, 'I wonder if all the windows are closed.'

'It's been raining like this the whole day,' says Father.

'Did you get wet?' she asks. 'You didn't take your umbrella today.'

'Not really, the whole day I was inside, in the office. Very very busy, I couldn't spend a minute at my desk, had to keep running around, ordering people to do this and do that.'

'I didn't do anything, just some cleaning, the kitchen shelves were very dirty.'

'Isn't that what we pay the maid for?'

'No, she's all right, just a bit sloppy. Anyway, it's good she leaves some things unfinished, helps me spend my time.'

'Don't you have better things to do?'

'I don't know.'

*

We can hear Father sigh, he turns, he's now facing Mother. I can now slide out from underneath the bed on his side and, because his back is turned away from me, I can breathe easy, even look around. I move to relieve the pressure on my knees and peer around. Father's toes stick out of the sheet, his back, big and heavy. There must be some crack in the pane which I cannot see since the drapes are moving now, letting light from the outside enter the room in a narrow rectangle which, luckily, falls just short of the bed, keeping my friend and I in the dark.

'When I went to pick her up today, the tea-stall owner, Mr Sarkar, was talking about the suicides.'

'That Sarkar keeps talking through his hat.'

'No, but people have died, ten to twelve, I think.'

'I don't blame them, given the hell-hole this place is. I would have killed myself long ago had it not been . . .'

'Had it not been for what?' Mother asks.

'Forget it,' he says.

'No, tell me, why did you stop?'

'I'm happy, why should I kill myself? People respect me. That man in the post office, the one who writes letters? Today, he asked me the spelling of a word. I helped him. You are happy as well, you don't have to work, sit around at home, you can do whatever you wish.'

'At times, I wish I worked . . .'

'Why, don't you have enough to do already?'

'No, I could get out of the house for a while, meet other people.'

'What would you like to do?'

'I don't know, my father once said I would make a good reporter.'

'You want to be like your father? You said you were always afraid of him.'

'I know.'

Father coughs once, twice, makes a sound as if he will get up from the bed but lies down again. On my left, in the light from the window, I can see a cockroach crawling towards the wall.

'I'm worried about her,' Mother says.

'What's there to worry about?'

'Did you read about the girl they found in the small town, killed and raped, lying at the bottom of a canal?'

'No, I didn't. But don't believe everything you read in the newspapers. They said last night there was an accident in which two trams collided. Imagine that happening.'

'She told me this morning she had a dream last night, a very bad dream.'

'What did she see?'

'That she was drowning in a glass of water, you were in the room reading the newspaper. She called out to you but you didn't listen, maybe the sound didn't pass through the glass or maybe it was too weak.'

'And how did she fit into the glass?'

'It was a dream. I think she's afraid. You can't blame her, someone she knows has died, some girl from her school. And then all the other deaths.'

'*She has nothing to be afraid of, both you and I are here, we aren't buying all that nonsense about the suicides. You tell her that. I will also tell her in the morning. I don't like her crying.*'

'*Yes.*'

'*And tell her to study. Every time I see her, she's reading her English book, something about describing people. She keeps drawing those faces over and over again, Rima and that man, what's he called?*'

'*Alam.*'

'*Yes, I hope she's studying other things, too.*'

The rain's hammering on the window. The pane creaks, the wind tugs at it, hard, trying to prise it free of the latch. Both Father and Mother are now facing away from me, lying like two inverted commas. He has a hand across her, lying there, still, the fingers over her breast. She doesn't move. He removes the hand, the cockroach is now against the wall, still.

'*I was looking at the album today, the photographs of our marriage, do you remember?*'

'*What?*'

'*It was raining just like it is today.*'

'*Was it?*'

'*We need a new album. The gum has dried off the old one, many of the pictures are about to fall off.*'

'*OK.*'

*

The wind enters the cracks in the windows, makes the plant rustle. By now, I can see everything, not just shapes in the dark but what they are of as well. I am even breathing easier now. I feel the planks, there is a small gap between two through which I can see the mattress, its grey cover, a tiny bit of it which has squeezed out.

'The rain, I don't know when it will stop,' Mother says.

'This is the rainy season,' says Father.

'Remember in the town I lived, just outside the city? If it rained like this, the roads would get flooded. I haven't been there for a long time.'

'What's there to go for after your mother's death?'

'Sometimes I think I should take our daughter there, show her where I grew up.'

'If you ask me there's no need to do that, she has enough to see already.'

'She would like to see the canal, it looks good when it is full of water.'

Father doesn't reply, she waits, he doesn't reply.

Are you awake, Mother asks softly.

There's still no reply.

Mother gets up from the bed, her footsteps make the cockroach scurry along the wall, it slips in through the closed door that leads to the balcony. She walks to the window, pushes the drapes aside and looks out. From underneath the bed, I can see her face lit by the light. She presses her face against the glass, my friend holds my hand as we both watch, from underneath the bed. We can see her cry, we can see the rain outside looking in, through the glass, smudged with dust and grime, at the water in her eyes.

She returns to bed, turns on her side, we hold our breaths and wait for her to fall asleep.

A story only for me

WE ARE BACK in my room now, sitting on my bed in the dark. It's got colder although the fan is switched off. I can hear the first birds waking up in the trees across the road.

My friend says he's in a hurry, he has to go now.

Are my parents safe? I ask.

Very safe, he says.

How are you so sure?

Didn't you see the pictures, didn't you read the words, didn't you hear them just now?

Yes, I say, but I don't understand.

Give yourself some time, he says, I will leave the pictures and the pieces of paper with you. Keep them carefully, whenever you are afraid, take them out, arrange them in whatever order you want and you will understand your parents' stories.

What stories? I ask.

Of the dreams your father and your mother have, the worlds they travel to, with their eyes open and their eyes shut. It's all there, in the pictures you saw and in the words you read and you heard, mixed up, jumbled, here and there, a bit of this, a bit of that.

What about me, I ask, will I be safe?

How can I forget you, he says, after all that you have

done? And that's why, my child, I've kept the last bit for you. What you are going to see will be your story, a story only for you and no one will know.

He gets up, I hear neither his footsteps nor his breathing. He begins to walk towards the door, with his hands in his pockets, his head lowered as if he were walking in a wind, raising his head only when he comes close to the door where he stands still, turns around, puts one finger of one hand to his lips, motions me to be quiet, absolutely quiet.

Then I hear a rustle.

A flap, a peck, a tap, it's a crow that has suddenly formed in the darkness, and through the gap in the door to the balcony, I see it sitting on the ledge. I have never seen a crow in the dark, its eyes glint in the pale light just before sunrise, and in this greyness, the crow's wings look blacker than black painted by the last brush of night.

It begins to peck at something, maybe an insect that was sleeping, a grain of rice that fell off Mother's dress when she came here tonight after clearing the table, after taking Father's half-eaten dinner away.

My friend now begins to walk towards the crow which keeps pecking, hopping in short hops, once in a while turning its beak to scratch itself under one wing. My friend climbs on top of the balcony's ledge, and as he begins to walk towards the bird, a strange little thing happens: he begins to grow smaller with each step, so that by the time he is halfway towards the crow, he's almost my height before shrinking further until he's like the doll I see in my favourite shop, and finally when he reaches the crow, he is just a few inches taller than the bird.

I stay seated on my bed, I don't want to walk to the balcony because I am afraid I may scare away the crow. So I have to strain my eyes to see him now as he gets up on the crow, looks at me, waves once, twice, says in a whisper that only I can hear.

Look at me, he says, look very carefully, I'm going to give you your own little secret, just like your father and your mother have in their pictures and their words.

And even before he can finish the sentence or wait for me to ask another question, the crow takes off. In a small circle at first, around the balcony, so that I can see my friend clearly, the bird's legs, curled up, pressed flat underneath its belly, my friend's legs, one on either side, in tiny trousers and tiny shoes.

He bends to his left to look at me, waves his hand. The bird is now high up in the air, I look up, the sky is clearing and both bird and man fly, away from the rising sun which is still below the horizon, its first light staining the black with a grey glow.

I stand still, afraid that what I see is so fragile that any movement I make, of body or air, will break it, make it disappear. But, no, that doesn't happen because when I close my eyes, open them again, the sky is turning a blue white and they are still there, my friend and the bird, high up, far far away, my friend a little bit raised so that the bird doesn't feel his weight.

I am now on the balcony, I keep looking, and as they get smaller and smaller, my friend and the bird, I feel tears lining up, drop by drop, just behind my eyes but I don't let them out, I don't want anyone to wake up to the sound of a child crying.

So I blink hard, the tears go away, back to where they came from. And through the empty space between the blue white sky above and my grey black balcony in front and below, over the rustle of trees and the first sound of birds as they sense the dying of the night, I can hear my friend say: I shall come to see you whenever and wherever you need me. These words ringing in my ears, his pictures and his scraps of paper in my hand, I look up at the sky again, I look straight ahead. And I look down, I am not afraid of heights.

EPILOGUE

Look at the picture on the cover, there's a child, a girl in a red dress; there's a bird, a crow in a blue white sky. And then there are a few things you cannot see.

THE END

I wish to thank:

David Knowles, of Ledig House Writers' Residency
in Omi, New York, for his incredible gift:
almost eight hundred hours of solitude

My agent, Gillon Aitken, for his faith

My editor at Picador, Rebecca Senior,
for her magic blue pencil

Shekhar Gupta, my editor-in-chief in New Delhi,
for a rare, dual privilege: letting me float in fiction and
remain anchored in fact. At a great newspaper,
The Indian Express

Dr Bal Krishna Mishra and the staff at his hospital
for helping me watch and hear

Pratik Kanjilal, for giving the book its name
when it was just a chapter old

To Elisabeth Iler, for her New York home and heart

And Sujata Bose, my partner. For everything